P9-CRE-372

A House Divided

For Dot & Bob,
With all my love,
Marj Durasich
1994

A House Divided

by

Marj Gurasich

A Chaparral Book
Continuing the Saga of
Letters to Oma

Texas Christian University Press
Fort Worth

Copyright 1994 © by Marj Gurasich

Library of Congress Cataloging-in-Publication Data

Gurasich, Marj.
A house divided/by Marj Gurasich.

p.   cm. — (A Chaparral book)
"Continuing the saga of Letters to Oma."

Summary: After one brother is killed by Confederate vigilantes,
Louisa, youngest daughter in a German American family
living in Texas, sets off to rescue another brother
from a Union prison camp.

ISBN 0-87565-122-4

1. United States—History—Civil War, 1861-1865—Juvenile fiction.
[1. United States—History—Civil War, 1861-65—Fiction.
2. German Americans—Fiction. 3. Texas—Fiction.]
I. Title.

PZ7.G98145Ho 1994
[Fic}—dc20

93-14189
CIP
AC

1 2 3 4 5 6 7 8 9 0

The cover illustration is based on a German traditional folk art
called *fraktur*. *Frakturs* were decorated and hand-lettered docu-
ments recording births, weddings, awards, and deaths. They often
contained such design motifs as hearts, animals, flowers and
vines.

Cover art and design by Barbara Whitehead.

A house divided against itself cannot stand.
Abraham Lincoln, 1858

In loving memory of

Stephen and Bob

Robin and Paul

Acknowledgments

No book is written in a vacuum; without outside help, most authors would agree, the book would be a sorry thing. My "outside help" came from all the librarians in whose libraries I did research. Without them I could not have found what I needed about the Civil War period to make this book come alive. I especially appreciated the use of that unsung hero of the library world — Interlibrary Loan.

Two men need special thanks for their help: W. M. Von-Maszewski of the Department of Genealogy and Local History at the George Memorial Library in Richmond, Texas, helped me locate little-known sources; and, without Gillespie County Historical Society's Hans E. Bergner's direction, I would not have known that the old church in Fredericksburg originally had two doors, not one as it has now.

And, once more, a huge thank-you to my two daughters, best friends and critics, Barbara Riley and Wendy Adair, for their much-needed support. They kept me going when I was discouraged and applauded the loudest when things went well.

And, again, thanks to Judy Alter, director of TCU Press. Being a writer herself makes Judy more understanding of a writer's ego-needs, and she is always there with a word or two of encouragement.

Prologue

Fredericksburg, Texas
November 6, 1860

Tina stood watching as shovelsful of sodden earth fell in the grave upon the pine coffin. The ceaseless rain beat its steady rhythm on the umbrella Papa held over them both.

"Goodbye, my darling Jeff," she whispered, closing her eyes against the tears.

When Fred had lumbered up the hill from the swollen, rampaging Bear Creek, carrying Jeff's limp body in his arms as though he were a child, she knew he was gone from her. She remembered screaming. Then everything went black until she awoke on her bed, the anxious faces of her family surrounding her.

"Are you all right, Tina?" Papa had asked, his old face strained and sad, his eyes full of compassion for Tina and sorrow for his own loss. He had loved Jeff as a son, even before Tina had married him. How long ago? Only twelve years. So short a time together. So short. . . .

"Come, Sis, it's time to go." Fred's soft whisper broke into her thoughts. She took her younger brother's arm as he gently led her away from the dark hole that held Jeff's body. She held fast to Papa's arm on her other side, his

1

faltering steps a reminder that he too would someday leave her, just as her darling Oma had the year the twins were two. And, just as Mama had, back in the winter of '47, right after Tina's baby sister, Louisa, was born.

Tina shook her head at the thought of Louisa. Thirteen now and such a tomboy! She'd rather tuck her skirts up and help Fred with the goats than learn all the woman's-work things she'd need to know someday. That's what came of growing up with nothing but brothers and nephews.

Louisa had always been a hard one to handle. I guess we all spoiled her, Tina thought, drawing her black wool coat closer about her and trying to hurry through the driving rain to the carriage. Mud clung to the hem of her coat and her best black silk moire dress. She took no notice, her thoughts turned inward.

Ahead on the rocky path out of the little cemetery Will walked with Louisa. Scowling now, as he always did when he was upset, he put his arm around Louisa's slim shoulders, almost at a level with his own. They didn't see much of Will anymore, since he had married Melissa and gone to live on her father's cotton plantation in far south Texas. Last week he had come to visit Papa and, when Jeff . . . when . . . when it happened, he had stayed over for the funeral. Tina's vision clouded, and she stumbled. Papa gave her elbow a squeeze as he steadied her.

"Daughter, we're at the carriage. Come, I'll help you up." Papa's voice quavered. He too had been lost in thoughts of his own.

"No, Pa, I'll do it," Fred said, quickly taking charge. Fred always saw to it that Papa didn't exert himself too much. He had grown frail these past few months.

"Everyone, listen," Fred called to the people milling about the carriages and wagons, huddled beneath umbrellas, trying to keep somewhat dry while they said farewells. "Y'all come to our house, now. The good ladies of

Fredericksburg have cooked up a wealth of vittles. It wouldn't do to let 'em all go bad, now, would it?"

"Yes, everybody, do come," Tina added, with only the smallest amount of shaking in her voice. "Come and have food and drink before you start home. Jeff would want it so."

The little caravan of carriages and wagons wound its way through the paths of the cemetery and headed down the road south of Fredericksburg for the Robinson place. Amidst the scrubby junipers and dark-trunked live oaks and overlooking Bear Creek, Jeff had built a sturdy, two-story house of native stone for Tina and his family. Tina often thought of her mother and how much she had wanted a home like this. Today she felt very close to Mama.

The friends and neighbors gathered in the big main room of Tina's home, chatting more easily now that the funeral was over, and enjoying the bounteous feast the women had prepared. Talk turned to this day's national election and what it might mean to Texas.

"Did you vote today?" each asked the other. Interest had run high for this election, people sensing its importance. Most of the men said, "Ja," a few, "Nein, what is the use?"

"If that baboon from Illinois, that Lincoln fella, is elected," boomed Will, "you hear my words, this country will split itself apart like a ripe watermelon."

"You mean secession?" Fred spoke up, his quiet voice commanding attention. "The southern states wouldn't be that foolish. An act of secession could only lead to one thing — war!"

A murmur swept through the room. Fred had said aloud what all were thinking.

"There's nothing to worry about," Will said, glancing at his younger brother with disapproval. "Lincoln can't win, nor that bombastic fellow, Douglas. It'll be Breckenridge, you can bet on it. But, I'll tell you this," he added, "Melissa's father says that if Abe Lincoln should by a strange quirk of fate be elected, the South will rise in rebellion. We're not going to let our states' rights be trampled."

"You mean, you'll not let anyone take away your slaves, don't you, Will?"

There was a stirring of assent to Fred's words among these mostly first-generation German-Americans who had, for the most part, never approved of slavery.

"Ja, Will," Papa spoke up, hoping his son might find a change of heart, "remember what Ralph Waldo Emerson said, 'If you put a chain around the neck of a slave, the other end fastens itself around your own.' It is not right, the owning of another human being, as though he were an animal or a piece of furniture."

"Papa, you just don't understand the business of raising cotton," Will said, protest in his voice. "Besides, we treat our servants well. We see to it that they have enough food, and we take care of them when they are ill. They are better off than they would be if they were free."

"Perhaps so, my son," Papa said, with sadness in his voice, "except for one thing. They are not free!"

Will turned away from his father, as though to deny the words he had just heard, his face scarlet and pinched. Tina knew that Papa used to be the only one who had any influence on Will's thinking — now there was Melissa, she thought. And Melissa's father, she added with a grim sigh.

Everyone started talking and shouting at once, Fred and Will looking as though they would come to blows any moment.

Louisa brushed past Tina on her way to the staircase.

"I can't stand it if they're going to carry on that same old argument," she complained to her older sister, her blue eyes flashing with anger. "I'm going to my room. I can't stand to hear any more of this old war talk. It's been going on for as long as I can remember . . . I'm just sick of it."

4

Tina watched Louisa run up the stairs, attracting startled looks from the guests. She shook her head. That girl's manners needed mending. She'd have to get after them right away.

Secretly, she agreed with Louisa. Slavery and states' rights had been the main theme of every get-together they had attended for many months. There seemed to be no answer. What would happen if this Lincoln should by chance win today? Would the southern states really leave the Union? Would it really mean war?

Ach, she thought, her mind reverting to German as it often did when she was upset, for now I must war with my rude and errant sister. She pushed her way through the crowd and ran up the stairs.

"Louisa!" she called, impatience in her voice, "Louisa Emilie von Scholl!"

Part One
Louisa Emilie von Scholl

Chapter One

Fredericksburg, Texas
April 25, 1862

"*Louisa!* Louisa! Hurry — Mama says come to the house!"

She heard her eleven-year-old twin nephews' voices before she saw them clambering up the steep hillside to where she sat.

"Louisa! It's a letter — from Uncle Will — after all this time! Do hurry! She won't let us hear a word till you're there."

The twins, whom Tina had named Sam Houston Robinson and Zachary Taylor Robinson after the Texas governor and the United States president at the time of their birth, were beside themselves with excitement. Louisa sighed, put the bottle with which she had been feeding the baby goat back in her basket, and slowly stood up. She tucked the little animal under her arm and carried the basket in her other hand.

A letter from Will? After so long? No wonder Tina was excited. They hadn't heard from their stubborn brother for nearly two years. Not since that awful fight between him and Fred and the others over "states' rights" and "the slavery issue" and all that bothersome business that had brought on this bothersome war.

Sam and Zach, their red hair glinting in the sunlight like new copper pennies, were on either side of her, tugging at her skirts, pulling her along, chattering all the while like two busy squirrels in a loaded pecan tree.

Louisa stumbled over the rocky hillside and down into the valley toward the large stone house, wondering about Will, who had stomped out of their lives on the day of Jeff's funeral. The same day Abe Lincoln became president — and everyone knew then that there'd be war! And now a letter?

The kid in her arms bleated, and she realized she was squeezing him too tightly. Poor thing, she thought, no mama and a nurse who nearly strangles you! I'll take you back to your aunts and uncles to watch over you, little fellow. If these clouts of boys will let loose of my skirt!

Louisa yanked at her skirt and almost fell as it tore free of the twins' hands. She set the baby goat down near a couple of older goats who watched warily, their long, curly hair glistening white in the shade of the live oak trees lining the steep path. The shy creatures bounded into the protection of the stand of trees, the little orphan bleating as it followed.

"Hurry, Louisa!" Sam called as he and Zach ran the last few yards to the house. Their excitement was contagious; Louisa found herself running too. The three of them tumbled into the house, breathless and laughing.

Everyone was there, that patient waiting look on their faces. Papa sat in his rocker by the window, holding his book open to keep his page. Fred sat close by, straddling a straight chair with his arms across the back.

Seven-year-old Emmy stood at Tina's elbow, waiting for a sip of "white coffee," as she called coffee laced with lots of milk. Carefully, Tina poured some from her cup and handed a small cup to her youngest child. Emmy gave Tina one of her dazzling smiles and took a long drink. When she put the cup down, everyone laughed.

10

"Emmy's grown a mustache!" Zach said, pointing.

"But it's white, not red like her hair!" Sam added with a snicker.

Emmy frowned and ducked her head.

"You boys stop teasing your sister," Tina scolded.

It seemed to Louisa that Tina was always scolding these days. She used to be such fun, laughing and enjoying a joke on herself. But since Jeff's death two years ago, she had turned in on herself and become quiet and . . . angry. Louisa had found the best way to handle that was to disappear and stay out of her older sister's way. That brought on more scoldings about shirking her share of the household work and not doing her part in the family. There wasn't any way around it, things had changed in the Robinson and von Scholl families.

And this awful war between the states — and the break from the family by Will — had made it so much worse.

"Come, sit, everyone," Tina said, her voice anxious. "Let us see what Will has to say after so long a time."

They sat in the heavy oak chairs around the big kitchen table. Outside of Emmy's slurping her coffee, there was no sound. All eyes turned to Tina who held the letter in her shaking hand. She looked at Papa, her children's Opa, and said, "Papa, with your permission I will read Will's letter, ja?"

Papa dipped his head in assent and drew deeply on his pipe. At least they could still grow their own tobacco for Papa's pipe, Louisa thought.

Tina cleared her throat. She seemed hesitant about opening the letter. She's probably afraid Will has decided to leave the family forever, Louisa thought. That would break Papa's heart. The rattling of the paper as Tina withdrew the letter from the envelope captured Louisa's full attention. She held her breath.

"The letter is dated February 19, 1862," Tina began in her school teacher voice. "He is at a place called Camp

11

Winston, in Texas." She looked around the room. "Will has joined the Army of the Confederacy!"

Eyes widened; Louisa gasped; Papa sighed. Fred hit his fist against the wall and muttered something, his face red with anger.

"Read what Uncle Will says, Mama," Zach said, his eyes bright with excitement. "Maybe he'll tell us all about the battles and the soldiers' guns and everything."

"*My dearest family,*" Tina read, squinting to read the faint pencil scratching on the thin paper. "*I know that it was with hard feelings and anger that we parted the day of Jeff's funeral.*

"*Today, though, our country is at war (the very war I predicted would happen if Lincoln got himself elected, eh, Fred?) and I could not, in good conscience, stand by and see our states' rights trampled into the ground. Lincoln would deprive us of our slaves and, in so doing, of our livelihood.*"

Tina stopped reading. Fred burst from the room, his face a study in anger and frustration.

"I can't read anymore," Tina said. "You read it, Louisa," she said, turning away.

Louisa straightened the paper where Tina had crushed it. She started to read.

"*I volunteered for the Army of the Confederacy on January 30 last year. I had been thinking about doing so for a long time, but Melissa kept telling me of my responsibilities at home on the plantation. Her father, though, said I had an obligation to the South and to cotton, that I should go. Finally, I could put it off no longer. I had to enlist and join a cause I so firmly believe in. We've had some hard times and have had heavy losses, for instance, when the Yanks took New Orleans, but I still feel sure that we will prevail. Bobby Lee is the best general there ever was. You'll see; the South will win and become an important country on its own, and those Yankees will wish they'd never heard the rebel yell!*"

Louisa looked up from the letter. Tina, unable to sit still and listen, had gone to the kitchen and was stirring cornbread batter for supper. She's beating it to death, Louisa thought, listening to the sound of the wooden spoon slapping against the bowl. Papa relit his pipe for the third or fourth time. Emmy had fallen asleep on the floor. Only the twins seemed enraptured by the letter, yearning for gory details of death and battle.

"Should I go on, Papa?" Louisa looked at her father, his face solemn.

"Ja, child, read on," he said, with a sigh. "I cannot imagine how Will could stray so far from what we have always believed. We Germans do not agree that one man has a right to own another. It's as simple as that! Will has forgotten everything his papa has taught him. It makes my heart sad to see it so.

"But, ja, read the rest of what he has to say, Louisa." Papa settled back in his chair; he closed his eyes as Louisa started to read.

"So now, my dear family, I am a soldier under our President Jeff Davis, and proud to wear the butternut and yellow. I hope that you will see your duty, Fred, and join me and our brothers in this great fight for our liberty. I hear it won't be long before the South orders conscription and then you will have to go, with no choice as to where or when, as you have now. Think about it, little brother."

"There's nothing to think about, big brother!" Fred yelled from outside the door. "I'll never fight to help those rich plantation owners keep their slaves. You'd do well to remember you are a German first and a southern slave owner second."

Louisa nodded in agreement at Fred's outburst, but she felt a sickness in the pit of her stomach. Their family would never get back together now. The rift was even greater than it had been for the past two years. She glanced

13

at Papa who seemed to have shrunk into himself. He, too, was realizing the great damage that had befallen the family, Louisa thought. In the kitchen, Tina slammed pots and pans about in frustrated anger. Louisa smelled the pungent odor of sauerkraut. When Tina became upset she always cooked Papa's favorite meals, as though to make up to him for whatever sadness he might be feeling.

With his outburst Fred had rushed back into the room where the others sat, stricken.

"Papa, I will never go to war to keep Will's slaves for him, or to worry about state's rights! I believe, like Abe Lincoln and old Sam Houston, in keeping the Union strong and all in one piece. If I have to fight, I'll join the boys in blue, I swear I will!"

Louisa felt a shudder race down her spine. Will fighting for the Confederacy and Fred for the Union?

She folded the pages of Will's letter and put them in the pocket of her apron. She couldn't finish reading it now. All of them were too upset to listen anymore. Maybe tomorrow. . . .

"Come, Papa, everyone," Tina called from the kitchen, "Supper is ready, come, sit, eat!"

Fred hurried to help Papa up from his rocker and the twins bolted past, their appetites ready for anything their mother cooked for them. They never noticed the shortage of food these days. Didn't Ma always have something on the table to fill their empty stomachs? Just now they were so excited to think that their uncle was fighting for the Confederacy, they hardly noticed what they were piling on their plates.

Emmy, though, took Louisa's hand, as if she sensed that things were not right but didn't know what could be wrong.

They all followed the twins into Tina's warm kitchen. For a little while they could pretend that the letter had never come and that everything was just as it should be. Maybe, even, for a few moments they could imagine that there was no war splitting apart a young country and a once strong and loving family.

The letter in Louisa's pocket reminded her how foolish their game of pretending was — the war was real and so was the heartbreaking split in the von Scholl family and nothing could change that.

Nothing.

Chapter Two

Papa leaned back in his chair, wiping his mouth with the huge napkin he insisted on using. To look at his grateful smile, Louisa thought, you'd think he'd had a feast, instead of our war-poor fare of sauerkraut and cornbread.

"Tina," he said, "danke schoen for the fine food this night." Then, with a long sigh, pulling out his pipe and ancient leather tobacco pouch, "Louisa, get out the letter, please, and continue. We must read it, all of it, no matter what pain it brings to our hearts."

Louisa drew the crumpled paper from her pocket and placed it on the table before her.

Her eyes scanned the letter until she found the place where she had stopped reading before dinner.

"Of course, Fred," Will's letter still addressed his younger brother, "you will want to do as I did, enlist in the state militia. Then you will be trained in Texas and will stay with the same group of fellows when enough join to make a regiment and go off to the war!

"I was lucky enough to be elected lieutenant by my fellow recruits and so have a fairly good life here in camp. Our rations are beginning to thin a bit, but we still have bacon and cornmeal. We also get a pound of molasses and a half pound of sugar for six men daily. It helps the cornmeal go down! Not like Tina's cooking, but it keeps a little meat on our ribs."

Louisa glanced at her older sister. Tina sat still, with no expression on her face. Only her clenched hands, their knuckles white, gave her emotions away.

"Well, dear family, it is time for curfew, and this candle is about burned out anyway. I'll say goodnight for now and hope to hear from you soon. I hope Papa is well and all are doing fine there.

"Oh, yes, I almost forgot. Do you suppose you could send me some lice powder? The little devils are everywhere, and Melissa has not been able to find any powder for me. I'd appreciate it. Between the lice and the fleas, we don't get much sleep at night.

"Think well on what I said, Fred. Come on down and join our company. We still have several spaces to fill before we can be listed as a regiment and get down to the real business of this war — killing Yankees!

"Your loving son, brother and uncle, Will."

Louisa folded the thin sheets of paper and looked up. No one moved or made a sound. Even Emmy and the usually restless twins sat transfixed.

Then Papa cleared his throat. All eyes turned to him — when Papa cleared his throat, he had something to say.

"I'm sure my son, Will, is sincere in what he is doing. I'm sure he believes in Jeff Davis and the Confederacy. But I cannot risk losing two sons to a lost cause. So, Fred, if you're considering what Will said about joining him. . . ."

"Papa, how can you even think such a thing?" Fred asked, hurt in his eyes. "You know how I feel about the war. I will not fight to keep the cotton planters happy and preserve slavery for them! No, I plan to stay right here and take care of our family and tend the goats and mind my own business. Let the southern plantation owners — and my brother, Will — fight their war if they want to. I'll have no part in it!"

A sense of relief traveled around the room. Papa moved from the head of the table to his favorite rocking chair and picked up a book of poetry. Tina carried dishes to the sink. Louisa and the twins took the rest of the table things to Tina. Emmy sat next to Opa, her grandfather, and patted him on the arm. She didn't understand what had been going on, but she knew Opa had been upset.

Only Fred remained seated at the big table. Head in his hands, shoulders slumped, he seemed to be pondering Will's words, probably wondering how the two of them had grown so far apart. Louisa watched her brother's agony and yearned to go to him, but she knew he had to work this out alone. He and Will had been the closest of brothers. Now, they were strangers. How sad, Louisa thought, as she dried and redried a platter until Tina took it from her and put it away on the shelf with a thud.

Everyone certainly was edgy.

Life settled back to normal, if anything during this terrible war could be called normal. Papa continued to read his newspaper, the *Neu-Braunfelser Zeitung*, whenever his friends there mailed it to him. The war news was getting no better for the Confederacy. How sure the southerners had been, at the start of the war, that they could finish off the Yankees in short order! And how wrong they had been. This was not to be a short war, as all had hoped, but a long, costly one with much hurt and tragedy on both sides.

So Papa told the family each night as they gathered around the table for Tina's "make-do" dinners. Luckily they had garden vegetables. Everything else was becoming very scarce. Louisa thought how much she would love some of Tina's fine *sauerbrauten* — or *weinerschnitzel*. But better not to think of such things. Better to pretend that Tina's vegetable soup or stew, without meat — unless Fred had shot a rabbit or squirrel — was exactly what she had been yearning for.

19

Louisa, who loved the outdoors, chose to help Fred with the care of the goats instead of doing household chores with Tina. Sam and Zach, not to be outdone by a girl, wanted to help Fred too. Emmy tagged along.

So it was, that on this particular sunny April day, all of them, except Papa and Tina, were in the hills surrounding the farmhouse when they found the fugitive. Fred was tending to a goat with a torn hoof, Louisa holding the animal so that Fred could treat it. She made little crooning sounds which seemed to soothe the animal and soon it was lying quietly across Fred's lap.

"You sure have a way with animals, Louisa," he said, approval in his voice. "If you were a boy, you could be an animal doctor."

"Yes," she said, with bitterness, "If I were a boy, I could do lots of things I can't do now! It's just not fair."

Fred put on his teasing voice. "Well, I reckon you could cut your hair and crawl into some men's britches and no one would be the wiser — you're sure tall and skinny enough to fool most folks!"

"Fred von Scholl, bite your tongue! It's not bad enough that Tina thinks I have to be a 'lady,' now you have to remind me that I'll never look like one, much less act that way."

In her anger at her brother, Louisa let go of the goat which took quick advantage and fled from the two humans holding him captive. Before Fred could stand up, the goat was gone into the rocky hillside where it might take days to find him again.

"See there, smarty, now you've done it," he said, but with a laugh in his voice. "You'd think someone could take a little teasing, wouldn't you?"

"It's not funny, my dear brother. You know how much I hate being a girl! A little, puny baby girl who caused her mother's death, got herself kidnapped by Indians and had to be rescued by her older sister! Tina has told me that story often enough!"

"Whoa, there, girl, wait up," Fred said, smile gone and a deep frown replacing it.

"You were not the cause of Mama's death. It was the virulent fever. Lots of folks died of it that year. And you can't blame Tina for wanting to retell the most exciting adventure of her life — she gets precious little of it now."

"I'm sorry, Fred," Louisa said. "It's just that I get so tired of thinking of what's ahead of me. Husband and babies, and washing and cooking and cleaning and drudgery! I want to do things that are important, that will make a difference in the world. You can't hope to do that, unless you're lucky enough to be a man."

"Well, you never know, little sister. You may have undreamed-of adventures, the likes of which the rest of us poor folks would give our horse and buggy and a fat milch cow for!"

"Now you're teasing me again, Fred von Scholl, and you know how I hate it!" Tossing her long hair, as golden as that day's sunshine, Louisa flounced off, away from the source of her anger.

She stopped and leaned against a tree, breathless. It was hard to flounce with rocks and roots and briars waiting to trip you at every step. As she caught her breath, she thought she heard a groan.

She stood still, listening. She heard it again. Louisa sucked in her breath and held it. When she felt near to bursting she let out her breath with a whoosh! Still no one had spoken or called for help. It was just a low moan. Perhaps an animal was hurt.

She started in a small circle, ever widening it, pushing aside the thick scrub to look for the hurt thing. She hoped it wasn't a bobcat — or a skunk!

She had made about six circles when she came upon the source of the noise. A man! Lying in a heap, face down, he looked more like a pile of old clothes than a man. Louisa waited for her throat to loosen enough so that she could call out.

"Fred! Here! Come, hurry!"

"I hear you, Louisa, I'm coming!"

While she waited for Fred to find her, Louisa bent over the man on the ground and tried to see what was wrong with him — without actually touching him. Cautiously, she circled him, watching for movement. But, when it came, it was too fast for her. A hand fastened itself around her ankle, nearly making her fall.

"Hey! Stop that! Let me go!" Louisa screamed, furious with herself for letting this happen, frightened beyond belief that the hand that held her belonged to one of the few unfriendly Indians left around these parts.

Beyond the hand and arm that held her, a head arose from the deep underbrush and thick grasses. The matted hair looked as though it would be as blond as her own, once it had a good scrubbing. She relaxed. No Indian. She could deal with some old renegade. Taking a deep breath she kicked at where she thought the rib cage might be and a loud yelp told her she had guessed right. The hand around her other ankle loosened and she jumped back, breathless with the exertion.

"What is it, Sis?" Fred came lumbering through the woods, the boys and Emmy trailing behind him.

"That!" Louisa said, pointing. "I haven't seen his face yet, but his hair is light. He's no Indian!"

Chapter Three

Fred grabbed the hand that protruded from the dense underbrush and pulled hard. Slowly, with much groaning, first a face, and then a body appeared.

"Why, he's just a young fellow, can't be more than sixteen, seventeen," Fred exclaimed. "Come, help me, Louisa. He seems to be hurt."

Louisa, feeling remorseful for the severe kick she had administered to the "young fellow's" ribs, rushed up to help Fred. Together they finally got him out and rolled him over. His face was badly bruised and blood oozed from a cut on his forehead. He seemed dazed.

Fred bent over and scooped the young man up in his arms and carried him off in the direction of home. Louisa hurried to keep up, the twins ahead of her, eyes alight with excitement, Emmy trailing behind.

At the house, Tina, drying her hands on a kitchen towel, rushed out to see what all the commotion was about. The little parade reached her just as Papa came through the door, a puzzled frown on his face.

"We found a stray!" Fred called, readjusting the young man's weight for the last few feet. Without a word, Papa held the door open and they all trooped through, Sam and Zach each trying to tell the story before the other.

"Hush, y'all!" Fred ordered. "Let Louisa tell Tina and Papa what happened. After all, she's the one found him."

The twins subsided, crestfallen. There wasn't often news of this kind to tell. They looked at Louisa, challenging her to tell the story better than they could.

"Well," Louisa began, "I heard someone moaning in the live oak grove and there he was, in the underbrush. Fred picked him up and brought him home."

Sam and Zach groaned. They could have stretched that story out to last at least ten minutes.

Papa cleared his throat. All eyes turned to see what he would have to say to the hurt boy.

"Tina and Louisa are pretty good nurses, son, so I think we can get your body back to health in no time, but we need to know some things first. Like who you are and where you're from and, most important, how did you come by all those cuts and bruises?"

Tina was already busy heating water and tearing bandages. Louisa brought a down pillow and an old quilt from the bedroom. The boys and Emmy fidgeted, alive with curiosity.

"Uh, well, my name . . . is . . . Helmut. Helmut Schultz, sir. From New Braunfels. Was on my way . . . " he paused to take a deep breath against the pain, "to stay with my uncle . . . "

"Oh, ja," said Papa, "that would be old Hermann Schultz, isn't that so? I know him well, a fine fellow, a fine cabinetmaker. I will send my son Fred to fetch him here." He gave a nod to Fred who quietly slipped out the door and headed for the barn to saddle their old horse, Buster, and ride into town.

"Danke schoen, you are very kind." The words seemed to come a little easier now as Tina gently washed the dirt from his bruised and cut face.

"Now, Helmut, tell us who did this to you." Papa's voice was quiet but insistent.

"I think it was the Waldrip Gang, *Die Haengebande*, they're called, sir," the boy said. Painfully, he pulled himself up onto his elbow. "At least, while they were beating on me, they kept calling me 'Yankee lovin' German' and worse names I couldn't repeat in the presence of these ladies."

Louisa shuddered. Papa had told them of the Hangman's Band.

J. P. Waldrip claimed to be a Confederate officer. His gang, according to Papa, was a band of riffraff, some probably Confederate deserters. They prowled the countryside, taking what pleased them, destroying what didn't, often hanging the poor victims who were guilty only of being German.

So far, at least until today, they had not ventured into the hills beyond Fredericksburg. Were they going to make this their next raiding grounds? Louisa's heart lurched at the thought.

Helmut was eating the chicken soup, without chicken, which Tina had made that morning, their last chicken having been eaten some time ago. The soup was mostly a few carrots and potatoes, from the garden, and noodles made with water and a little of their precious flour. At least, it was hot and smelled good; Tina had used one of her last bay leaves for flavor. Louisa shook her head in wonder. Tina had learned how to make much out of nothing.

When would this war end? How would they live through it, if Waldrip and his "hangmen" were to hurt or even kill Fred? She couldn't bear to think of it.

Helmut's uncle, the cabinetmaker, brought his team and wagon and with profuse thanks for "such kindness rendered," carted Helmut off to Fredericksburg. After they left, the family gathered around the kitchen table. It was time to face facts. If the Hangman's Band had been on their land, or near it, Fred was no longer safe.

As Tina poured what passed for coffee, Papa cleared his throat.

"The situation is more serious than we might think, my son. The newspaper, which Hermann Schultz kindly brought me with our mail, and which is already over a week old, has bad news. Conscription! All men between the ages of eighteen and thirty-five are ordered to report for duty at Fredericksburg immediately, to be sent to the nearest militia headquarters. Anyone disobeying the law will be shot as a traitor!"

"Oh!" cried Louisa, her eyes wide with fright. "It can't be possible. The Confederacy wouldn't do such a mean, cruel thing!"

"I'm afraid you're wrong, little sister," Fred said, bitterness in his voice. "I've been hearing rumors in town for awhile now. It was only a matter of time before all the men in Fredericksburg are called to the war."

"But, I'm not going! I refuse to fight the rich plantation owners' war when my family need me here at home to keep body and soul together."

"But, what will you do, Uncle Fred?" Zach asked, all the usual teasing and banter gone from his voice.

"I've already given it some thought," Fred said. "We'll all keep an eye out for Waldrip's men, stand regular watches, and if they come, I'll hide in the little cave on the north hill. No one outside of our family knows about that cave. I'll be perfectly safe until they leave. After a while they'll get tired of coming way out here for nothing."

Louisa was the first to react to Fred's words. "We'll take blankets and a lantern and some food out there, in case you have to stay overnight, Fred. It's a wonderful plan, and I think we should get busy right now. Who knows when those horrid men will be back?"

"I'll take first watch," Sam, who had been very quiet, said. "I'll sit up on the north hill where I can see anyone coming onto our property."

"I want a watch, too," Emmy spoke up. "Uncle Fred, can I have a watch? I'll learn to tell time ever so fast."

26

Fred and the others laughed. "Yes, little one, you'll get a watch, someday. It'll be the kind that tells you what time of day it is, instead of telling you whether the enemy is coming!"

The laughter, as always, relaxed them and put aside their fears for a little while. Louisa remembered stories that Tina had told her of the early German immigrants and how hard they had to struggle to survive in Texas. Their laughter often saved them from despair, often pointed the way to better times. She would need this heritage to help her through the bad days ahead.

Chapter Four

Weeks went by, the family always on guard, fearful that Waldrip's gang would discover Fred's hiding place. Twice they ranged through the hills, cursing and shouting at the "German scum" to come out and "fight like men."

One day in May Papa read from the *Neubraunfels Zeitung*. "Listen to this, everyone, 'General Paul Octave Hebert, the commander of the Military Department of Texas, has declared martial law in Gillespie County and troops of the state militia are being sent into Fredericksburg, ready for possible trouble.'

"Ach, now it will be harder to keep Fred safe. Troops will be everywhere." Papa put down his paper and wiped his forehead. His hand was shaking.

"Don't worry, Papa," Louisa said, "we'll double our vigilance. No one will ever find Fred!"

Papa seemed relieved for the time being. But, soon there was another danger. His name was Captain James Duff. He commanded an irregular Confederate unit called Duff's Partisan Rangers who were worse than Waldrip's Gang had ever been. Duff declared that "Dutchmen are Unionists to a man," and "I will hang all I suspect of being anti-Confederates."

Louisa lived in fear that Duff's men would find Fred and take him away — or worse — hang him. Sometimes they burned houses of people they only suspected of harboring a "Dutchman," as Duff called the German protesters. Men fled the area by the hundreds, hoping to get away from this persecution.

Fred refused to leave. He spent many hours and days holed up in the cave that had once been the twins' favorite play place.

Now it was nearly August, time for the Angoras to be sheared. Fred announced that the work of harvesting their fall crop of mohair should be started right away.

"Let it go," urged Papa. "You are sure to be captured if you climb through the hills gathering up the goats. Besides, who will help you? All the young men have gone — either to the Confederate Army or running away from it."

"I'll help," chimed a chorus of voices. Louisa, the twins, even Emmy all crowded around Fred, talking at once, urging him to let them help him.

Fred and Papa finally compromised. Louisa and the boys would bring the goats in, one or two at a time, to the cave where Fred would clip them, while the others kept watch. If Duff's men came near, Fred would retreat to the back of the cave until it was safe again.

For days they worked, shearing the precious mohair from the Angora goats. Soft and white and curly, the goats' wool would bring a good price if it could be smuggled past the Yankee naval blockade into Mexico.

"The cotton farmers are hauling their cotton to Brownsville," Fred told his father, "then ferrying it across the Rio Grande to Matamoras on the Mexican side and getting more money than they ever did before the war. The British and French ships are lined up, waiting to take a load back across the ocean. Think what they'll be willing to pay for our fine mohair! We'll be rich!"

"I don't like it," Tina said, after a long silence, "it is too dangerous. Besides, what would we do with all that money? There's no longer anything to buy! No clothing, no shoes, no food — I don't know what we'll do if this war keeps on much longer. The twins and Emmy continue to grow, war or no war."

"We just can't afford to waste this opportunity," Fred argued. "Mohair is our only cash crop. The war will be over one day, and we'll need the money then. The British and French pay in gold, not Confederate paper."

Louisa looked at Fred, adoration in her eyes. He was so brave, so smart. His blonde good looks had made many a Fredericksburg girl's heart beat faster, Louisa knew, because some of them were her friends and confided in her. But he had no time for girls. With that old German work ethic Tina always was harping on, he had time only for work, work, work.

"I think you should go, Fred," Louisa said. "And," she continued, "I will go with you!"

Quickly, before the expected objections could be voiced, she went on, "You'll need help along the way, someone to spell you as driver while you get some sleep, someone to see that you eat."

"Ridiculous!" It was Tina who spoke up first. "Whatever are you thinking of, Louisa? It would add double danger for Fred to have a girl along on the trail. I won't hear of it!"

"I wasn't going to be a 'girl' on the trail, Tina," Louisa said, striving hard to keep her emotions under control. "Fred gave me the idea. I'll cut off my hair, wear a cap, dress in some of Fred's old clothes and go as his young hired hand."

"Never! I won't allow it! Whoever heard of such a thing?" Tina looked at Louisa as though her younger sister had gone mad.

"Now, Sis," Fred spoke quietly, but with a special gentleness in his voice as he smiled at Louisa, "you know

I was just teasing you — I never meant you to take me seriously."

Louisa shook her head and started to speak. Fred put his hand on her shoulder. "I want to thank you, Sis, for wanting to help me. But, you know you're needed here. You have to take charge of the goats and watch out for the twins and Emmy. You also must take care of Papa," Fred continued, "and help Tina all you can. See how much I'm depending on you, Louisa?"

Fred hugged his tall, slim sister, whose eyes were clouded with tears and whose voice seemed to have lost the ability to be heard.

"That is *gut*, Fred," Papa spoke up. He had been watching the little scene without speaking. "You are right, and we all thank Louisa for staying here to help us. Is it not so, Tina?"

"Of course, Papa," Tina said, her lips pinched together. She rubbed her hands down the sides of her apron and turned toward the kitchen. She did not look at Louisa.

So it is always going to be, thought Louisa with a growing sense of dejection. Always left out of the excitement because I'm a girl, always left behind. Oooh, if I were only a man. I'd show them all.

"Opa! Mama! Someone comes! Fast!" The twins peered out the window in the growing twilight to see who approached the house. "It's just one man. Couldn't be Duff — those cowards never ride alone."

"I'll go see who it is," Fred said. He opened the heavy door and stepped out onto the stone porch. Louisa crowded the boys at the window, eager to see who the visitor might be.

"It's Helmut Schultz! Old Hermann Schultz' nephew that Louisa rescued." Zach had recognized him first. "Maybe he's come a'courtin', Louisa." Zach nudged Sam in the ribs and they both roared with laughter. Louisa decided to ignore them, which left them disappointed.

"No one comes a'courting at a full gallop, Zach," Tina put in as she, too, watched the rider approach the house. Fred stood at the foot of the porch steps, waiting.

"Hello, Mr. Fred," Helmut said, his fair skin turned pink in the wind. He jumped down from his horse and hurriedly hobbled him. "There's news I thought you ought to know, so I rushed right out." He stood uncertainly, twisting the old-fashioned German cap he had been wearing.

"Well, come on into the house, Helmut, and welcome back," Fred said with a friendly smile. "You look some better than the last time we saw you."

"Ja, I am fine now, thanks to all of you, and especially, Fraulein Louisa." The twins jabbed each other in the ribs. "I come with news from Fredericksburg. You have heard, I guess, about the conscription?"

Heads nodded, but no one spoke. Helmut continued, "The governor has written that anyone not willing to give the oath of allegiance to the Confederacy has thirty days to leave the state — or be shot as a traitor!"

Slowly, struggling with the unfamiliar words, he went on.

"Many of our men do not wish to join the army, or to fight in this war. They want only to be left alone. But, now it is impossible for them to stay here any longer. They must leave or be killed. They are getting together to go to Mexico under the leadership of Major Tegener. They will take supplies and ammunition and plenty of packhorses so that the trip will not be dangerous or difficult. When they reach Mexico some will join the Yankee army and go north to fight. Some will stay there and wait for this war to end.

"I want very much to go, but I am not yet eighteen, so not in danger of . . . what is the word? . . . conscription. Major Tegener says I can help more by staying here.

"Fred," Helmut's face was red with the exertion of talking so much, "the men are going to meet on the first of the month at the head of Turtle Creek, you know, in Kerr County. They want you to go along. You must get away, for your own safety and the safety of your loved ones."

A stunned silence followed Helmut's words. Finally, Fred spoke.

"My good friend, I will follow old Sam Houston's example. He, too, refused to take that oath because he believed the Union should be saved at all costs. Besides, I will not be pushed out of my home and made to run like a deer before a hunting party! I am going to take my chances right here, with my family."

For the next several minutes the sound of excited voices bounced off the walls of the stone house. Each person had a different argument, until at last no one remembered who was for or who against Fred's leaving.

It was Papa's quiet voice that finally convinced Fred.

"Last week," he said, "Anton Runge was found hanging from a live oak tree, his home burned to the ground. Only the little three-year-old girl survived the fire.

"Those renegades show no mercy and now we must also fear the army and conscription — perhaps prison as well! I believe it would be safer for all of us if you would go with Major Tegener, my son. Wait in Mexico where you will be safe. At the end of this horrible war, you can return to your home and family."

In the silence that followed, Louisa looked at her brother. He looked so calm and so brave. I could not stand it, she thought, if anything ever happened to him.

"Well, Fred," Louisa said, trying to make her voice sound light and unworried, "you'd better get ready for your trip to Mexico!"

"I guess you're right, little sister," Fred answered in his slow, deliberate way. "We'll pack up the mohair we have ready and hide it in the cave. The rest of the goats will have to wear their heavy coats till I return. Then I can sell all of it at once."

"Ja, my son," Papa said, "I think it is right that you go. Surely this war will be over soon. Our hearts will be heavy until your safe return. You will write us as soon as you arrive safely in Mexico, ja?"

"Yes, Papa, I will write."

Three days later, after many goodbyes had been said and hugs given, Fred joined Major Tegener and about eighty men from the surrounding areas. They checked their supplies and ammunition and were on their way to the Mexican border, looking more like they were on a friendly camping expedition than an expedient escape.

Louisa watched the line of mounted men until they were out of sight. She wondered when she'd see her beloved brother again.

Although Louisa did not realize it at the time, Helmut Schultz, nephew of the Fredericksburg cabinetmaker, would make the waiting and worrying less painful, the time less slow moving. He rode up to the von Scholl-Robinson house one day, hobbled his horse and walked, somewhat hesitantly, as far as the steps of the porch. There he stopped, cap in hand, and looked up at Louisa who sat in Papa's rocker, watching his unusual behavior.

She realized that she had never really looked at Helmut before. Tall and slim, his face was thin and angular, unlike the German boys Louisa knew in town who tended to have flat, wide features. He reminded her of a willow tree; the wind could bend it double, but it would not break. She noticed his long, slender fingers as he fidgeted with his cap, waiting, it seemed, for a word from her.

"Hello, Helmut," she said. "Come sit up here, in the shade, and rest awhile. Would you like a glass of water? I'm sorry I can't offer you lemonade!"

"Is no matter, Miss Louisa," Helmut said with a shrug. "We have no lemonade, either, or anything else of the old days, for that matter. I just wanted to come for a moment, to tell you that I feel for you . . . about your brother . . . uh . . . a great worry. I hope he is safe . . . for I know how much pain you are feeling . . . uh . . . I have lost loved ones. . . . It is . . . very hard."

"Oh? You lost someone in the war, Helmut?" Louisa asked, interested for the first time in learning more about this shy, young man.

"Nein, not in the war, Fraulein, but in Germany, before I come to New Braunfels — and then, to my uncle here in Fredericksburg. My father and two older brothers died in an explosion in the plant where they worked in our town in the old country. My mother died, of pneumonia, two years later. . . ." Here Helmut paused, his narrow face pinched with the painful memories.

"Helmut," Louisa said, reaching out to touch his arm, "I am so sorry. You lost all of your family?"

"Ja, it is so. Then I took the little money from the sale of our small home and came to America, to Texas, to cousins in New Braunfels. They came upon hard times, so they sent me to Uncle Hermann.

"It is here that I have been happy . . . the most happy in the last three years. Uh . . . you and your family helped bring me to this happiness, Louisa." Helmut's pale face took on a rosy shade and he lowered his eyes.

"That is why," he added, softly, "I wish I could do something for you, now in these hard times with your family. Ja, if there is ever anything I can do, you have only to ask. Please remember this, you will promise me, Louisa?" The last words were spoken in such a low tone Louisa had to lean forward in her rocker to hear.

"Thank you, so very much, Helmut," she said, a catch in her voice. "You are very kind. There is nothing anyone can do for us. We can only wait. And that is so hard, it makes me want to jump out of my skin!"

36

A smile crept over Helmut's face, crinkling the skin around his blue eyes, softening the angles of his face.

"When I feel like that, Louisa," he said, "I play my violin. It calms me. Do you have such a way to help you?"

"No, Helmut, I don't. Except to work, work, work."

"Tell me about your violin," she said, to change the subject. "I didn't know you played an instrument. Did you learn in Germany? Will you play for us sometime? Papa is a great lover of music."

"Uh . . . I am not too good the violinist, but I would be proud to play for you and your family, Louisa, if it would give you pleasure.

"Now I have bothered you long enough. I must go. But if it is all right with you, I will come again very soon. And . . . and, ja, I will bring my violin."

Helmut backed down the steps, his eyes never leaving Louisa, and mounted his horse. With a small gesture of goodbye, he rode back toward Fredericksburg.

Louisa sighed. The silence was even more oppressive after Helmut left. She wondered how soon he'd return and play for them . . . for her?

Louisa did not have long to wait. Two days later, early in the morning, Helmut was back — a little shamefaced at coming so soon — and carrying a battered violin case.

To cover her own embarrassment, Louisa called out, "Everyone, come! Helmut is going to play his violin for us! Hurry!"

"We come, daughter," Papa said as he emerged from the darkness of the house and blinked at the sunlight. Like bears leaving their den after a winter's sleep, the twins and Emmy came, rubbing their eyes. Tina followed, brushing her hair back with the palms of her hands.

Helmut's face grew red and his hands shook as he took the old violin and its bow from the case. Without a word he tucked the instrument under his chin and drew the bow slowly across the strings.

For the next few minutes, magic reigned. The clear, fluid notes of Helmut's violin caught each listener's heart as the music flowed through the morning air. Papa's face lit up as Helmut played the old German tunes, one after the other. Tina's toe tapped out the rhythms, until she raised so much dust she started to cough. Louisa watched Helmut's narrow face, violin tucked under his chin, as he lived the music which his bow produced, seemingly without effort.

Finally, perspiration glistening on his forehead, he lowered his bow to his side and looked up at his audience for the first time since he had started to play.

First came a sigh, then applause from everyone, then a shout of "Bravo!" from Papa.

Helmut looked at Louisa, searching her face for a reaction to his performance. She smiled and clapped until her hands hurt.

"That was *wunderbar*, Helmut," she exclaimed, using one of the few German words she had bothered to learn, to Papa's despair. "You must be tired. Come, we have some sweet potato coffee in the house . . . ugh!"

Laughing, she grabbed Helmut's hand and pulled him toward the house. The twins snickered and pointed to Louisa and Helmut and nodded their heads. We told you so, they seemed to be saying.

The next week passed pleasantly. Louisa and Helmut took long walks in the afternoons, after chores were done for the day. Louisa had quit searching for more work to do and was content to finish her regular jobs, then to relax in Helmut's company.

Sometimes she packed cornbread and some pears from their wild pear tree and the two of them would go up the hillside for a picnic. They found a limestone cliff where they could sit and let their eyes roam for miles over the rocky countryside. Louisa loved this land people called the Hill Country.

One day Helmut had his violin with him and he sat facing the limestone cliff across the ravine and played music he had never played for the family. Sweet and sad, the sounds made Louisa want to weep and smile at the same time. She closed her eyes and let the music sweep her along. Even when it stopped she sat still, eyes closed, listening to the echoes of those last notes.

Her eyes flew open as she felt a soft, sweet warmth touch her lips. Helmut's eyes were closed as he kissed her, so he didn't see the surprise in hers. Then, suddenly, she was enjoying the kiss, and returning it. Now it was Helmut's turn to be surprised. His eyes opened, wide, and his head jerked back.

"Ach, Louisa, I am so sorry!" he blurted. "What could have come over me, to be so bold?"

Louisa laughed and took his hand. "Don't worry, Helmut, I liked it. I'm glad you kissed me. Would you like to do it again?"

"Er. . . . ah . . ." Helmut stammered. "Nein, Louisa, I have too bold already been. I must go now, ja?"

Louisa smiled to see how Helmut's English suffered when he was embarrassed.

"Well, you will come again, won't you?" she asked.

"Ach, if you will say so, Louisa, ja, I wish to, very much."

"Then, you must. And soon," she added, a twinkle in her eye. She was enjoying Helmut's discomfort. It made her feel very grownup and wise.

Chapter Five

The days crept by slowly, as waiting days always do. Louisa pretended to be very busy, but her heart wasn't in any of her chores, or in the conversation Papa and Tina tried to keep going. She often thought of Helmut and his unexpected kiss, a thought that brought a flush to her cheeks and a small smile to her lips. But that remembrance was her only unworried thought and it was quickly replaced by that nagging fear for Fred's safety.

While they waited to hear from Fred, Louisa decided to answer Will's letter, the letter which had upset them all so much that Tina had put it in the bottom of her dresser drawer and no one had mentioned it since.

Louisa didn't need the letter to remind her of Will's words, even though they had received it months ago. Her mind ached with the memory of each sentence, each word. She wondered whether her brother might be dead on some unknown battlefield . . . or if he was still playing at soldiering with the state militia in Texas. All she could do would be to write him at the last address they had.

She sat on the stone steps of the house and gazed out on the land before her. Shimmers of August heat wavered over the parched grass; even the trees looked thirsty. It would be awhile before the cooling rains would come, then sometimes they came a gullywasher. Then the

Pedernales and Guadalupe and other rivers would rage with flash floods — the kind that took Jeff from them on their own Bear Creek. She remembered how he had been hurrying along the dry, rocky river bed that day, chasing a runaway goat when a raging wall of water, as tall as a man, crashed down the ravine, carrying everything in its path. Jeff never had a chance.

Louisa shook her head. It was time to think of today, not yesterday. She frowned with the effort to concentrate on her letter.

"Will," she wrote, her pencil a mere nub, "*if you are still in Texas, I hope this will reach you. If they have sent you on to fight somewhere, my prayers may find your heart, if this letter does not.*

"*I regret that we have been so long in writing you. Your words were of such a shock to all of us, we could not talk about them among ourselves, or think of trying to write a reply. But the war goes on and much has happened. I thought it right to let you know how things are with us, even though I must confess I am still angry with you for joining the rebel army!*"

Louisa put the tip of the pencil between her lips and tried to think of what to say to Will. How to tell him what his letter had done to Papa, who now moved and acted like a very old man, carrying the weight of his unhappiness and worry over his eldest son. How to tell him of Tina's pinched face, her eyes sad and angry at the same time. She still could not accept the fact that Will had forgotten everything Papa had taught them, of man's equality, each to the other, and the importance of living your beliefs. And how could she tell Will that his brother had daily risked his life to stay with his family and try to protect them? That Fred even now was on a perilous journey? A journey from which he might not return. . . .

Louisa felt the anger building. She tried to hold it back, to hide it. Suddenly, there it was, denied for so long,

42

welling up within her, an anger such as she had never felt before. She wished that Will were there and she could beat on his chest and scream and cry.

"*I cannot express myself well in a letter, Will,*" Louisa wrote, her spirits sinking lower and lower as her anger increased, "*only, I cannot forgive you for making all of us so unhappy and disappointed in you. I cannot forgive you for joining up with those rebels whose beliefs and ideals are so different from what Papa taught us. I hate you for making Tina cry and Papa old and Fred so angry he no longer can speak your name. I hate you for no longer being the big brother I loved and trusted. I hope I never see you again in this world, Wilhelm von Scholl! Louisa.*"

Her skin wet with perspiration, hair plastered to her wet scalp, Louisa sat dejectedly, exhaustion taking over the sense of haste she had felt while flinging her words of anger at her brother onto the paper. Then, like the flash floods after a long, dry spell, the tears came. For once she did not fight them, but let them run down her cheeks in rivulets, dropping onto her dress, making deep sapphire streaks on the pale blue chambray. Healing tears, taking some of the anger away, replacing it with a deep sadness. For a long time she sat, thankful that the family had all gone to town with Papa and that only the mockingbirds and the crows could see her acting like a baby.

Finally she got up, wiped her eyes on her petticoat, and went inside the dim house. Squinting at the sudden change from bright to dark, she folded the letter and put it in the envelope she had fashioned out of another piece of wrapping paper. She crept to Tina's room and found the letter from Will, quickly copied the address onto her envelope and sealed it with a bit of candle wax.

She'd have to find a way to sneak it into town and mail it off to Will. She wondered if he would ever receive it — almost wishing he wouldn't, then defiantly hoping he would.

I hope he reads every word, she thought, and that he feels as miserable as I do this very minute!

But the longer she waited to post the letter, the harder it became to send it to Will. Maybe it was enough to have written it, she reasoned. Maybe I shouldn't mail it at all. Will probably has problems enough without my ranting and raving at him.

The letter remained in her apron pocket.

The sun was low on the horizon when the family returned from Fredericksburg, alive with stories of their day, all talking at once. Louisa was glad no one thought to ask her how her day had been; she might have broken down and told them her secret, about her letter to Will. The envelope lay hidden deep in the pocket of her muslin apron. The emotions of the afternoon had left her curiously empty and detached. She heard the twins and Emmy banter as though from a great distance, then realized with a start that Tina had called her name — more than once?

"What is it, Tina?" Louisa said, going into the kitchen where Tina stood looking at a pitifully small arrangement of groceries on the table.

"Look at this!" she said. "This was all the food we could gather together in Fredericksburg! Everywhere were long lines of *hausfraus* waiting to see if butcher or baker had something to sell or barter. Most did not. The situation gets worse every day. I do not see how we can go on much longer."

"Lucky we are, Tina, to have the garden!" Louisa reminded her sister. "Without our vegetables we might really go hungry!"

"Ja, and what do we do when the garden is done for the year? It is August already and soon will be frost and

44

the end of our vegetables. Then what, I want to know?"

Louisa shrugged. "Maybe this war will be over by then, is it not so, Papa?"

"Ach, my daughter," Papa said, his eyes shaded so that Louisa could not read them, "it is hard to say what will happen. The newspapers are not too happy with the way things are going for the South, but who can know when it is all so far away?"

An awkward silence fell as Papa gave a tired nod and turned to his pipe, losing himself in the tobacco.

Louisa caught hold of Sam's collar as he raced past her, chasing Zach. "Whoa, boy," she ordered. "Stop a minute and tell the stay-at-home some news. What is heard from those who left with Fred for Mexico? Has anyone heard anything at all?"

Sam twisted loose but stood still, rubbing his neck where the collar had tightened in Louisa's strong grasp. "I don't know a thing about it, honest, Louisa."

Unable to stand still a minute longer the twins burst into action and left the door wide open as they raced outdoors to let off steam.

What could happen anyway? Louisa thought. Fred and the others are only obeying orders, to leave the state within thirty days or join the rebel army! And they chose to leave. So what could happen?

She turned to go back to the kitchen and help Tina with dinner preparations. Why was there still a trace of fright inside her secret self? She shook her head, hard, to send those feelings scattering and called, "I'm coming, Tina," although Tina had not said a word.

The days dragged by, no word from Fred, no word from any of the men gone to Mexico. Louisa decided to try her hand at shearing some of the goats Fred didn't get to finish when he left in such a hurry. Anything, she thought, to get out of the house.

She sent the twins up into the hills to search out an unsheared goat and waited for them at the cave where Fred had spent so many hours and days.

She wondered about Fred. Where was he now? She prayed he was safe. But, what if the men had been discovered and turned over to the rebels? Fred could be hanging from the limb of a mesquite tree this very minute! Her scalp crawled, thinking of Fred in danger. She had to fight to keep her voice steady as she greeted the twins who half-crawled, half-slid down the steep incline to the cave entrance. Between them they dragged a very unhappy small Angora goat, protesting all the way.

"Come on, you smelly thing," Louisa coaxed, her voice soft to soothe the frightened animal. "Don't bother trying to use those beautiful, sharp horns on us. You are only going to get a haircut, nothing more, and think how much cooler you will be without your fur coat!"

"Louisa," Zach said, giggling, "you talk to those goats as though they understand you! I'm glad no one hears you but Sam and me, or they would think you daft!"

"Not at all, my so smart nephew," Louisa answered as she laid the goat on its side and knelt beside the young animal. She grabbed its feet and managed to pin them between her knees.

"See how he looks at me, how trusting he is, lying so still. He knows I will not hurt him. Now, hand me the clippers and we'll see if I can do this job as well as Fred would, if he were here."

If Fred were here . . . Louisa bit her lip and forced her mind away from her brother and back to the job before her. Carefully she clipped the soft, curly white hair from the young goat. This was its first clipping, and she was very careful not to cut the tender skin as she worked upward from the stomach to the back. Then, motioning for the boys to help her, she flipped the kid onto its other side and started over again.

46

It would have been easier had this been the winter shearing. Then a "cape" was left unclipped on the goat's back to keep it warm during the harsh winter. But now, in August, she had to do the whole job and her back ached as she finished and released the small goat who scampered away without a backward glance.

"He could at least have said, thank you," Louisa complained, a self-satisfied smile on her sweaty face. Ooh, how I must smell, she thought, as she plucked white strands of goat's hair from her wet skin and messy clothes. The goat looked a little patchy where she had missed a few spots, but, all in all, it wasn't too bad a job, for her first.

"I think Fred would be proud of me," she said.

"And, of us!" the boys chimed in unison.

Two weeks had gone by since Fred and the large band of dissenters under Fritz Tegener had left Fredericksburg. Worry and uneasiness lived with Louisa and her family every day as they waited for word that Fred had arrived safely in Mexico.

One morning as the family gathered in the kitchen, finishing a skimpy breakfast, they heard a shout and a knickering of horses.

"Ho, there, Herr von Scholl," Hermann Schilling cried, leaning far out from his driver's seat in the wagon filled with family and dogs. "Have you heard the news? There has been a terrible deed done, and we go to a secret meeting in town at the old church. Come, get your family and go with us!"

"What deed has been done, Herr Schilling?" Papa called to his neighbor. "And how can you have a secret meeting if all hereabouts gather together in so public a place as the church, right on the main street, between the courthouse and market square? Could any place be less secret?"

"That's the beauty of it, Herr von Scholl," Schilling replied to Papa's second question, leaving the first hanging in the air like wash on a line. "We pretend to hold church service, singing hymns for the soldiers to hear, then quietly attend to the business at hand. They will think we are praying. Come, come, there is no time to be lost talking. Gather your family together and follow us."

Without another word, he flicked his whip in the air and the draft horses started up, jerking the old, flat-bottomed wagon along behind them. The Schilling children hooted and waved; the outing was a welcome change of routine for them. They did not know or guess what news awaited them at the old *Kaffee Mühgle* or Coffee Mill church, called that because its octagonal shape and cupola on top reminded people of a coffee grinder.

Papa turned back to the house, calling to the twins who had followed the Schilling wagon out of the yard. "Come, everyone, we must go to town and find out what this bad news can be."

The twins rushed outdoors to make the wagon ready for the trip. Louisa hurriedly found her sunbonnet and helped Emmy into her pinafore to cover the mud stains on her only dress. Tina brushed her hair back from her face and rolled her sleeves down to her wrists. Ordering the boys to put on their shoes and comb their hair, she then busied herself putting together a lunch basket.

The trip, so often taken with leisurely enjoyment, today seemed to last forever. When, finally, the eight-sided church came into view, Louisa felt relieved and at the same time frightened.

An undercurrent of fear and tension swept through the church as neighbor talked to neighbor, all asking the same question, "What is it? What is this terrible news we are to hear?"

No one had an answer as the men and boys parted to enter the church through one set of doors and the women and girls gathered to use the matching doors on the other side of the central window. They seated themselves on the women's side of the church; the men were already settled on their side.

Louisa's eyes searched the opposite side of the big room until she saw Helmut standing in the back. She was glad he was here.

First, Martin Luther's famous hymn must be sung:
Ein' feste Burg ist unser Gott,
Ein' gute Wehr and Waffen,
Er hilft uns frei aus aller Not,
Die uns jetzt hat betroffen.

A mighty fortress is our God,
A good defense and weapon;
He frees us from distress and need
That has us now o'ertaken.

Then Ferdinand Doebbler walked to the front of the anxious crowd and began to speak.

"My fellow German friends, loyal Americans, one and all, I can hardly bring myself to tell you what I must, to cause weeping and sorrow among you, to send you home heavy of heart and fearful of what tomorrow will bring to our small community." He paused and wiped his face with a large blue handkerchief.

Louisa and Tina exchanged worried glances. What could it be that Herr Doebbler, the tavern-keeper, had to tell them that would cause him so much consternation? He was clearly shaken to the bone with it. Could it be something about Fred and the others? Something so terrible Herr Doebbler had trouble in the telling of it?

Louisa twisted her handkerchief in her lap as the boys and Emmy fidgeted, but Papa sat very still, waiting.

Chapter Six

Ferdinand Doebbler stood, uncomfortably rigid, before the room crowded with his fellow German Texans. His gaze roved from face to face, nodding at this friend and that, clearing his throat, standing first on one foot then another. Clearly he was finding it hard to begin.

"Tell us, Herr Doebbler, what has happened?" a voice from the back of the hall called. "Ja, tell us!" echoed around the octagonal room.

"Ja, my friends, now I tell."

Louisa thought she had never seen anyone so burdened, so sad.

"Remember," he began, "when our friends started out for Mexico two weeks ago?" Heads nodded. "Word has come to us about a battle between those unfortunate fellows and Duff's villainous band of so-called Confederate soldiers."

Gasps and small shrieks of dismay followed this announcement, but Herr Doebbler ignored them.

"Here to tell you the story as he lived it is our neighbor and friend, Wolfgang Dammert. He has just returned from the battle site."

Louisa and Tina exchanged worried glances as Wolfgang Dammert rose from a seat in the front row and slowly made his way to the pulpit. Head down, shoulders slumped, he obviously had no good news to impart. He cleared his throat and glanced around the crowded room as though to gather strength from all those expectant, uplifted faces.

"My *gut* friends," he began, his English deteriorating in the face of such stress, "a sad story it is that I must tell you. As you know, a large group of us Germans left here for Mexico on August the third. Our leader was Captain Fritz Tegener, a fine fellow, but too trusting. We should have known not to trust that Captain Duff when he said we had thirty days to leave Texas. We should have made our horses to fly through the woods instead of playing at camping as we went along, singing around the fire at night, enjoying our little expedition!

"Ach, what a bad mistake that was — many good men are dead because of it."

"Wolfgang, please," someone in the front row yelled, "get on with it. What happened?"

"Oh, I am sorry, my friend. It is just that I find this very hard to talk about, so I take all the way around it before I speak.

"We had traveled only as far as the Nueces River by the ninth of August. Captain Tegener said we would bed down for the night and perhaps spend the next day, it being a Sunday, hunting and enjoying ourselves before continuing on our journey. Some of the men said they would search the woods for beehives and we would all enjoy the sweet taste of wild honey by evening."

He shook his blond head, a frown on his face. "Herr Schwethelm opposed these plans, as did some of the others, saying we should hurry on and get many miles between us and the Confederates before we could afford to relax our fears.

"Fritz Tegener laughed and told them not to be such worriers. Did not the law say we had thirty days? But, he said, if they wished, we would leave the next morning and not unsaddle our horses until we crossed the Rio Grande. This seemed to satisfy those who had complained.

"We bedded down for the night, planning for the long trip ahead and the safety we would find across the border.

"Ach, it was not to be so." Here Wolfgang broke down, weeping like one in mourning.

"My friends," Wolfgang Dammert said in a choked voice, "I cannot go on." He wavered, as though to fall, then righted himself as he looked beyond the crowd to the open doorway. With a half-wave of his hand, he said, "Ah, here just returning is my good friend and companion in this terrible ordeal. Ja, he can tell you the rest. You must forgive me . . ."

With those words he stumbled back to his seat, drew a large blue handkerchief from his shirt pocket and loudly blew his nose.

All eyes turned to the doorway and the man leaning on the door frame. Louisa gasped. The morning sun behind him lit his silhouette, his face remained in shadow. But there was no doubt in her mind.

"*Fred!*" she called out, jumping to her feet and pushing her way past the seated people in their aisle until she reached her brother. She threw her arms around him, tears flowing unashamedly down her cheeks.

The rest of the family rushed up and there were many hugs and kisses while the rest of the congregation looked on, many with mixed emotions. They were happy for the von Scholls . . . but . . . where was their son, or brother, or husband? Where were the rest of the men who had left them so confidently nearly two weeks ago?

Slowly Fred left his family and uncertainly walked to the front of the church. Still in his ragged and dirty clothes, looking haggard, he stood before the crowd of his friends and neighbors and took a deep breath.

"About three o'clock in the morning we awoke, hearing shots nearby," he began. "Two of our guards rushed into camp — the other two, Beseler and Bauer of Comfort, had been killed! We all grabbed up our guns and stood ready to repulse the expected attack. But nothing happened. For hours our minds were in a whirl of anxiety, not knowing what to expect. At dawn we learned what was in store for us. Our enemy, who turned out to be Duff and his scoundrels, had encircled the camp, hidden by the cedar brush. When they were ready, they let loose a volley of shots straight into the center of our camp. We heard Duff's voice yell, 'Charge 'em, boys, charge 'em! Give 'em hell!'"

Some of the Germans, listening to Fred's story, stood and yelled their anger, stamping their feet and shouting to everyone within hearing distance to "get that rotten Duff and string him up to the nearest tree!"

"Quiet, quiet," Herr Doebbler urged, standing on a chair to make himself heard. "We are supposed to be at prayer, remember? Even with the doors and windows shut, as they are, such shouting is sure to attract the soldiers' attention!"

The noise immediately stopped, creating a loud silence that screamed in Louisa's ears. The ones in the crowd who had made all the commotion sat down, quiet but with angry faces. Sweat poured down their cheeks and necks, and big kerchiefs sopped up the dampness, caused by both their anger and the August heat trapped inside the closed building. One of the women grew faint and water was brought in to revive her.

Now, all was in order again and Fred proceeded.

"We answered the rebels shot for shot, but were at a disadvantage. Our campsite was in a fairly open area, while they remained obscured by thick cedar bushes. The firing on both sides lasted for about an hour. We were outnumbered three to one, and, worse, we used muzzle-loading guns, while the rebels had Sharp breech-loading rifles.

"Friends were falling all around me, some dead, many wounded." Fred bowed his head and, after a long pause, continued. "There was no time to see to them. Some of our company escaped, but finally the rest of us knew we must either give up or retreat. We would never give up to Duff and his rebel friends!"

Here a few men shouted, "Good men! Hurrah for you!"

"No, my good friends," Fred said, a catch in his voice, "it was not good! We had to leave many men, some beyond anyone's help, others, the wounded, who should have been cared for or carried away. There was no time. We helped the wounded who could walk and left the rest with our prayers."

Tears streamed down Fred's face now; he seemed not to notice. Fighting to keep his voice steady, he went on, "We could not take them with us. It was terrible . . . terrible. . . ."

For a long moment a wall of frightened silence surrounded each person in the room. No one could ask the questions tearing them apart, "What happened next? Did the wounded escape? Who . . . who died on that awful day?"

"Fred, my son . . . tell us . . . the rest of it . . . please." Papa, in his quiet way, urged Fred to go on.

The sweat rolled down the sides of Fred's ashen face; his voice faltered. Louisa held her breath.

"The wounded who could walk went first and we kept firing at Duff's men as we retreated. They did not follow us. We stopped soon and rested and waited for the rebels. But they did not come. All was quiet for a long while . . ." Fred's voice trailed away and he stared off into space. He shut his eyes against whatever vision he was seeing.

"Later we heard gunshots from the direction of our old camp, and we decided the rebels were celebrating their victory over us poor Germans. How I wish it were so, my friends . . ." Fred stopped talking, seemed even to stop breathing, a pale ghost standing before people so paralyzed with fear they could make no sound.

"We made our way back to the battlefield after there had been no sound for several hours. We hoped to help the wounded and to bury our dead. . . ." Great racking sobs shook Fred's entire body. He turned away from everyone and tried to compose himself. Louisa could hear women sobbing and moaning, women whose husbands or brothers or sons had been on that ill-fated trip . . . too afraid of the answer they might get, to ask the burning question: Is *he* all right?

"Every one of the men we had left on the field, too wounded to be moved, every one . . . killed . . . murdered . . . by those devils of Duff." Fred choked on the words which would break so many hearts of those good people who sat, stunned with shock and grief, before him.

"I never wish to see such a thing again," he said, sobbing. "I will never go to war or lift a gun against another human being so long as I live!"

A long silence followed Fred's words. Then sound burst from everywhere at once.

"It was a massacre!" shouted Herr Doebbler, "*a bloody massacre!*"

The whole crowd wept as one person, some of the men cursing in German, the women wailing and moaning. Louisa and Tina fell into each other's arms, their tears mingling as their cheeks touched.

Papa stood, braced himself for a moment to get his balance, then motioned to all of them, von Scholls and Robinsons, to follow him. It was time to go home. They would come back to help their grieving neighbors later, but now they should be left alone with their grief for lost, loved ones.

In silence Fred, nearly fainting, hung onto the arms of Tina and Louisa. The twins and Emmy followed Papa to the wagon and they all started on the solemn drive home.

Behind them, inside the little church, the German-Texans began to sing.

Herr, segne uns du,
Gib Frieden und Ruh'
Behut' uns von allen Gefahren!

"Lord, bless Thou us,
"Give calm and peace,
"Protect us from all danger."

How thankful she was, that Fred was at home and safe, Louisa thought. She could not imagine how it would feel to be in that church right now, not knowing if he lived or died! And thank God, too, that Helmut had not gone . . . that he, too, was here and safe!

Now if they only knew where and how Will was . . . was he well or hurt, alive or dead? No, it was too much . . . she could not think of that right now.

Chapter Seven

Papa watched the newspaper for every detail of war news. That is, he watched whenever a newspaper made its way into his eager hands. More and more often, the papers cut back on production due to lack of paper or ink. Sometimes transportation bogged down or the mails were late.

"What is the world coming to," Papa complained to Tina, "when a man cannot get his paper to read? Ach, I could almost as soon give up my pipe!"

Having said that, Papa settled back to read aloud his most current copy of the newspaper, adding his own comments to anyone who would listen.

He doesn't fool me, Louisa thought. He watches the papers for news of Will; he hopes somehow to hear about his eldest son. He would never admit it, though. Watching her father closely, Louisa saw him aging daily. Every day that brings no news of Will, Papa gets a little bit older, she thought.

The letter came one day when Papa was feeling especially low. Tina and the twins had gone to town, searching for "something, anything we can eat." They brought very little back in Tina's basket, but Zach waved the letter like a banner. News about the war! Maybe about battles Uncle Will had fought. The twins fidgeted while Tina put up her sunbonnet, stacked the few groceries in the pantry and looked around to see if everyone was present.

With a nod, she motioned for the letter. Zach gave it up willingly, waiting now to hear the contents as Tina read aloud.

"The letter is headed, *'The Second Texas Infantry, Tupelo, Mississippi,'*" she read. "*Dear Ones*, it begins."

Louisa glanced at Tina, wondering what her thoughts were. Tina's face had taken on a blank look, hiding her emotions. "*Dear Ones*," she repeated, swallowing. "*It has been some time since I wrote you last.*

"*So much has happened since then — and so little. I have been in the service of our dear Confederacy now for months, and not a day of combat have I seen! Only march and starve, march and starve, drill and wait, drill and wait. It is not what I expected when I joined the army of the South! I joined the Second Texas too late for Shiloh. Many of our good men died and many here are still nursing wounds from that battle. I must be patient — my day for fighting will no doubt come and I will try to bring pride to the South and live up to the expectations of all my dear ones, you, my own family, included.*

"*I am lucky to be a lieutenant. Besides other privileges, I have been paid my $85 a month regularly. Not so for the foot soldier; he makes only $11 a month and our fellows have not received a penny for eight months. I try to find out why and if they will be paid soon and all I get for reply is 'No money for the soldiers yet.'*

"*Conditions for the ordinary private are very bad now. His clothes are in tatters; many are without shoes and wrap their feet in rags. With no money to buy anything, a soldier must keep the darning needle going and hope his supply of thread holds out. There is no more thread to be had in the South, nor needles or pins. Melissa writes that she counts her pins every night and will not go to bed until she has every one safely pressed into her grandma's old silk pincushion.*"

The corners of Tina's lips curved upward enough so
that Louisa knew she was inwardly smiling at the thought
of the elegant Melissa down on her hands and knees,
looking for pins!

*"Despite the shortages of everything from pins to pickles,
I'm right proud of the Texas Second. You know, old Sam Houston's son, Sam, Jr., was at Shiloh with our outfit. Early in the
fighting he discovered the bible he had carried into battle had a
bullet hole in the back cover!*

*"Then in early April young Sam was severely wounded on
that battlefield. He would have been left to die, except for a
Yankee chaplain who discovered his name and had once met,
and liked, his father, old Sam, when he was a U.S. Senator in
Washington.*

*"Just before I joined them here at Tupelo, they were camped
at Corinth. Later, the end of May it was, General Beauregard
decided to evacuate Corinth, heading south to Baldwin. Our
men were greatly outnumbered, so that foxy Beauregard put
wooden guns — they call them Quaker guns, because they don't
do any fighting! — in the emplacements, manned by stuffed
dummies. During the night several trains pulled into town,
with the men cheering and band playing — all to fool the Yankees into believing replacements had arrived! It wasn't till noon
that it finally dawned on our northern friends that old Beauregard
had outfoxed them and gone!"*

"Gee whillikens!" Zach shouted, bringing Papa's head
up in a snap.

"Doggone!" Sam hollered, "those blue coats have to
get up mighty early to outwit our boys, huh, Ma?"

Tina's face took on a look of utter dismay.

"Hush, you two! You've scared your poor grandpa
speechless! And, watch your language there, you hear? I
won't have you sounding like you never had any bringing up.

"What's more," she continued, her face splotched red
with anger, "neither side in this terrible conflict can be

called 'our' boys. We are neutral. We do not believe this war should have been waged, but, since men don't have enough sense to settle their differences peaceably, we have to suffer for it. But we don't have to go along with them.

"Am I right in what I say, Papa?"

"Ja, my daughter, very right. Except that I might add, our beliefs more nearly match those of the North than those of the South. We believe in preserving the Union and we abhor the idea of slavery. So, if we were pressed, I guess we would have to say that the North should win this conflict."

"But, Opa," Zach cried, "what about Uncle Will? He is with the Confederate Army. You cannot want his side to lose!"

"That is what pains me, my grandson," Papa said, with a deep sigh. "How I wish Will had not been so quick to join the rebel cause. I perhaps could have made him see our point of view, if I'd had more time to convince him."

"No, Papa," Louisa spoke for the first time. "I think Will's mind was made up when he was here. Nothing we could do or say would have changed what he had to do. Just as Fred is doing what he believes is right."

Thank goodness I didn't mail that dreadful letter to Will, she thought. I understand him a little better now.

"Our family is not the only one divided by this war, Papa," she continued, "I have heard of several families in Fredericksburg who have had the same sadness befall them. And I'm sure there are many divided families in the North, if we only knew them."

"Ja, Louisa, you are probably right. I must remember to keep that thought in mind when I get low in spirit. We are not alone in our sadness. And, one day, this terrible war will be over, and perhaps we can mend all the fences and put our lives and our country back together again."

Tina and Louisa exchanged glances, neither being sure this hope of Papa's would ever be fulfilled.

"Should I finish the letter, Papa? There is just a little more."

"Please, Tina, do. We need to know all," Papa said, settling back into his chair once more.

Louisa moved quietly to the kitchen table and lit a lamp, then brought it into the seating area where the family was gathered. Dusk was settling outside and soon the inside of the house would be in total darkness. Tina waited until the comforting glow of the lamp spread its circle about them, and then she continued reading Will's letter.

"*Yes, my dear family, the Second Texas is a proud outfit. Those boys did themselves well at Shiloh — so well we now have the word 'Shiloh' on our battle flag!*

"*Many good men have died, or been wounded, but more come to take their places. I am proud to be with these brave men. I hope you, Papa, and all the rest, are proud of me, too.*

"*With all my dearest love to you all, Will.*

"*Post Script. Thank you, Tina, for the lice powder. It finally caught up with me.*"

"Tina!" Louisa said, her voice sharp. "You sent Will the lice powder? How could you, when we were all so angry and upset with him?"

"I couldn't let our brother suffer from those little creatures. It makes me shudder to think of it! I packed up the lice powder we had here and sent it to Melissa, who sent it on to Will. Was that so awful?"

"Well, I guess not," Louisa said, "but it would serve him right to have a few lice nipping at him, after what he has gone and done to our family!"

"I don't know why you say that, Louisa," Tina answered, her face pinched and angry at Louisa's criticism. "After all, didn't you write him a letter? Eh? What have you to say about that, Louisa?"

Louisa flushed, her whole body tingling.

"You saw my letter? Where is it? Give it to me at once!"

"Oh, I mailed it for you. I found it on the kitchen floor one day and, since it was our day to go to town, I posted it for you."

"You mailed it? How could you? It was my private letter to Will, and I had decided not to send it to him, after all. Now you've ruined everything with your meddling, Tina!"

"You shouldn't write words that you might regret someday," Tina answered, anger making her voice tight and hard. "But, don't worry, Will doesn't mention getting your letter — perhaps he never received it. Most letters don't reach their destinations these days."

Will may never forgive me for my awful words, Louisa thought. He may never want to speak to me again! Why did I ever write that letter in the first place?

She turned without speaking and went outside, pausing on the front porch. Inside, no one spoke for a moment, everyone feeling the pain of the sisters' argument.

"Well, I cannot sit around here twiddling my thumbs." Tina finally broke the silence. "There is much work to be done. Zach, Sam, we need water. Hurry, before it gets too dark. Emmy, you hold the door open for them when they come back — that's a good girl. And, Papa, there is a little of our ground pumpkin 'coffee' left, if you want it."

The next day, sitting at the mouth of the cave where Fred had hidden so many times and where she came often to be alone and think, Louisa looked out over the steep hillside with its outcroppings of granite and limestone. The live oaks and mesquite trees had turned gray with August's searing heat and blowing dust. As she wiped her forehead with the tail of her petticoat, she thought of the unkind things she and Tina had said to each other. Is that what this war is doing to us? she wondered. Our family divided and fighting among ouselves?

Trying to think of something less painful, she pondered Will's letter.

He certainly didn't seem to be taking the war too seriously — with his stories about fooling the Yankees and the like. But, of course, he had not yet seen any fighting. He still thought war was a game that strong men played, not the ugly, tragic thing Louisa thought it to be.

He has probably been in less peril than Fred, she thought, startled. How she yearned for the days before the war when she and Fred and the twins and Emmy spent happy days in these hills, chasing the smelly goats and singing and laughing.

Would those times ever come again? Could she and Tina mend their rift? Could Will and Fred ever be loving brothers again? Or would they all be too changed when this war was over to recapture that carefree happiness?

Chapter Eight

Days followed days and melted into months. Suddenly the air took on a crispness; mornings held a promise of cool days to come, days with bright, blue skies followed by nights half-lit by a cold, frosty moon.

Louisa had always loved autumn. The smell of it, the briskness, the colors. . . . It was a time of preparation; soon winter would be upon them.

On the surface it seemed the same. Whenever it seemed safe for him to be out of his hiding place, Fred and the twins cut firewood and stacked it against the house. Tina and Louisa hurried to dry the last of the vegetables in the waning sunshine. They made trip after useless trip to town, searching for foodstuffs, for medicines, for shoes and clothing, even for pen and ink and paper and stamps for mailing letters to Will.

"You'd think the government could get us some stamps, wouldn't you?" Tina complained as she rubbed her sore feet after another frustrating day in Fredericksburg. "They keep promising — but nothing happens.

"Can you imagine, Papa, there are no silver coins in town for change when you make a purchase! Herr Braun at the general store had to give me a slip of paper in the amount he owes me . . . a due bill. When he still had them, he used to give us a paper of pins as change. Wouldn't Melissa be green with envy, Louisa?"

The two sisters smiled at each other, their hurtful words becoming less and less painful as time passed. Tina continued her angry tirade against the never-ending shortages and high prices the war was causing.

"And who can pay the price they want for shoes these days?" She took up where she had left off. "The last ones we bought for the boys melted away in the first rainstorm! The soles were *paper!*"

"Patience, daughter," Papa said, trying to calm Tina. "We are lucky to have our little garden, our cow and the goats. You and Louisa are clever with the needle. Look how you made my old broadcloth coat over for Zach and turned the collars and cuffs on my worn shirts. The war will be over someday and things will be like they were before, ja."

"I don't think so, Papa," Louisa spoke up. "I don't think things will ever be the same here or anywhere in the South. I listen when you read your newspapers aloud. I hate what I hear — so much anger and bad feelings. Can it ever be healed? Can our own family heal, once the war is over? Can it, Papa?"

"Ach, Louisa," Papa said with a deep sigh, "who is to say? I hope it can be so."

So autumn had come, with its bright leaves and shining blue days. But nothing was the same, Louisa thought sadly. Nothing would ever be the same.

The one bright side to that worrisome autumn was that Duff's Raiders seemed to have gone elsewhere with their killing and plundering. No one had seen them thereabouts for weeks now. Louisa was glad, for it gave Fred more time to spend out of the hiding-cave, and he used it to good advantage. The house and barn were winter-ready. The woodpile reached to the second story of the house, and a mountain of kindling twigs stood beside the neatly cut and stacked wood.

Fred put extra hay in the barn for Bossy, the cow. Once in a while they even had a small amount of butter! Louisa had fashioned a small churn from an empty jar and an old thread spool on the end of a stick for a dasher. She skimmed the cream from the milk for a couple of days and was able to churn enough butter for everyone to have a taste. Oh, it was good! The twins and Emmy licked the knife after spreading it on their hot cornbread. With new cabbage from the garden boiled with a few of the red potatoes they had stored away, they had a fine meal.

Most missed was sugar — and coffee, of course. Papa would have paid dearly for a cup of good coffee. Tina tried everything to devise substitutes for these two favorite items, but with little success. Sorghum molasses was most often used for sweetener; occasionally the cotton farmers brought back coarse, nearly brown sugar from Mexico, but the prices were too high even to consider. Tina ranted over the "robbery" of the merchants who charged the poor people so much for items which were once everyday staples.

As for coffee, Tina and Louisa watched the newspapers for recipes for substitute coffee. They suggested using everything from rye and okra seeds, dried and parched then ground, to corn, sweet potatoes, acorns, cottonseed, peanuts or beans. Papa and Fred voted for okra seed coffee as the best. Tina had dried and saved all the seed from their sparse crop of okra, but it would never last the winter.

Seed for the garden became a problem too. They carefully dried and stored all the seeds they could from this year's garden, because there were none to be bought for next spring.

"The whole world has disappeared from the South," Louisa said one day. "We have nothing. How could we have been so foolish as to think we could win a war when we cannot feed or clothe our soldiers properly, or our homefolks either!"

Papa shook his head, his bushy, gray eyebrows knotted in a frown, his pipe forgotten for the moment. Fred's reaction was to storm from the house and attack the garden patch, trying to force the winter vegetables out of the ground and onto the dinner table.

Soon all the complaints and worries about the wartime shortages would disappear from their thoughts. Tragedy has a way of putting things into perspective. Little things are forgotten when real trouble strikes, as it did that October.

First came the letter from Will. He had left Tupelo, he said, and marched back to Corinth, now a federal garrison. The Confederate plan was to retake the city which was a fortress with a huge supply of Yankee supplies which needed to be destroyed or confiscated.

Will's letter, short and hard to read, had no mention of Louisa's letter, much to her relief. It ended with the hope that his family in Texas would pray for him as he went into battle, his first of the war.

Louisa shuddered as she thought of her eldest brother fighting Yankees. No other word came from him, but Papa followed the news in his paper, whenever the publisher could get one out, and at first it was good.

"General Van Dorn said, in a telegram to Richmond," Papa read with the others straining to hear every word, "'So far all is glorious, and our men behaved nobly.'" Louisa breathed a sigh of relief.

"Our loss," Papa continued, "I am afraid, is heavy." Frowns of worry creased the listeners' brows.

"Don't worry, Opa," Zach said, patting his grandfather's shoulder. "Our Texas boys will show those Yankees!"

The Second Texas, Will's regiment, fought gallantly, according to Papa's paper, against terrible odds. When the fourth color bearer of the day fell before the Yankee Springfield rifles, Colonel Rogers, Will's commander, siezed the banner and rode back to rally his men to yet another attack. With a shout, they followed him as he held the colors high. When they reached the ditch, where the cannons were placed, in front of the fortifications, the colonel jumped the ditch on his horse and dashed up the hill. He then planted the regiment's colors upon the fort. The men yelled in glee and swarmed around the fort and over the top.

The twins were breathless, fighting every inch with the Texas Second, smelling the gunsmoke and the sweat of the men — the temperature was a record ninety-four degrees, according to the report — and hearing the rebel yell as Will and his soldier buddies overran the fort that day.

Then, the paper continued, the Yankees brought in replacements and charged with everything they had. Hopelessly outnumbered, Colonel Rogers waved a white handkerchief in surrender. However, some of his men did not see it, and continued firing. In the return fire, Colonel Rogers was slain. The men fell back, still in possession of their precious regimental flag.

Papa looked up from the paper to the solemn faces surrounding him, listening with their hearts as well as their ears.

"Is there any more, Papa?" Fred asked, almost in a whisper. Louisa could not look at her brother; his stricken voice told her how he suffered.

"Ja, my son," Papa said. "There is more." He began to read again. "Both northern and southern newspapers give unanimous praise to the Second Texas Infantry, to Colonel Rogers and his brave men. Only four men in the entire regiment remained alive, three of them wounded, all taken prisoner. . . ."

A sob escaped from Papa's throat, and he turned his face away. Silence held the little group around the table, a silence made of horror, anguish and fear. Only four left alive? Could, by any miracle, one of them be Will?

71

The twins, their ideas of war's thrills and excitement gone forever, tried valiantly not to cry. They gulped and dug their grimy fists deep into their eyes, then both shoved their chairs back and ran outside.

Louisa and Tina sat stunned, their minds unable to go beyond the horror of the story they had just heard. Fred, tears streaming down his face, stood and put his hands on Papa's shoulders. There were no words . . . only the same thought in everyone's mind.

What had become of Will?

Louisa stood staring out the window, listening to the rain. It must be nearly midnight, she thought, watching lightning cast its eerie glow over the horizon. Far away, thunder muttered. The rain, absorbed quickly by the thirsty soil, splattered on the steps and porch of the house which suddenly seemed too big, too lonely.

Funny, she thought, Will hasn't lived here for years, yet the house and all of us in it miss him as though he had just left us.

She could feel guilt stalking her again, and she tried to think of something else, quickly, before it took hold of her as it had so frequently since Papa had read that article to them. Too late. Guilt washed over her like the rain streaming over the roof of the house.

If only she hadn't been so quick to write Will that hateful letter! What had she said? "I hope I never see you again in this world"? How could she have been so cruel to her own brother? Didn't he have the right to his own beliefs, just as she had?

She no longer blamed Tina for mailing the letter; she would have done the same. But what she wouldn't give to have that letter back in her hands, unread by Will, so that she could tear it into shreds, the way her heart was being torn now!

A House Divided

The rain had subsided to a steady drizzle. Louisa, her mind still aching with sadness, crawled back into bed, to lie staring into the darkness, awake for the rest of the night.

Thank goodness, there was lots of work to do! Papa said that working hard helped assuage the pain of sorrow. And guilt, too? Louisa wondered. She threw herself into a frenzy — cleaning the house from top to bottom till everything shone, raking the ground around the house — so that snakes and varmints could be spotted before they got too near, spading up the old garden and planting their few seeds for winter crops of cabbage, rutabagas, onions and parsnips.

Louisa followed Fred up the hillside and helped with the shearing of the goats, this time leaving their winter capes on them. Carefully, they packed the mohair into bundles for the trip to Mexico.

"You're working yourself to death, Louisa," Fred said one day after they had sheared a dozen or so goats. "Look how thin you are! You can't change what has happened to Will by killing yourself. It is not your fault! Will did what he wanted to do."

Fred was right, of course, but it didn't help. She felt as though all smiles and laughter had been taken from her, never to return, the way youth never comes back after old age sets in. She felt old, but how could she be old at fifteen?

If only she were a man! The old complaint again. If she were a man, she would go in search of Will, find out if, miraculously, he could be one of the four who had survived that terrible battle at Corinth and were now in a Yankee prison somewhere. If she were a man, she would not stop until she found him, or at least the truth about him.

But, she was not a man. And what could a fifteen-year-old girl do, except clean the house like a mad woman and shear goats . . . and think dark thoughts?

Chapter Nine

Later that week, as Louisa helped Fred with the shearing of more goats, she daydreamed about Helmut, his music and his kiss. Pleasant thoughts to scatter her fears for Will. Her mind was far away from the smelly goat she held, or the sound of the shears clipping the mohair in a steady rhythm. She didn't hear, either, the sound of a horseman stealthily approaching, until the clipping sound stopped suddenly and she felt a tenseness in the air.

She looked at Fred then, and fear took hold of her as she saw his face. She turned to see what had made him look so alarmed. From between the two mesquite trees nearest the trail down the hillside she saw a man, dressed in ragged but recognizable Confederate butternut uniform, astride a huge gray horse, his rifle pointed at Fred's chest.

Louisa gasped. The goat, sensing the human's lack of interest in it, escaped up the rocky hillside. Fred got to his feet, but Louisa was paralyzed with fear. She could not move.

"Who are you?" Fred demanded. "What are you doing on my property?"

"I came a long way to get rid of another Yankee-lovin' German. Colonel Duff and us have been huntin' you for a long time, mister. You better say your prayers, 'cause your day has come!"

"No!" Louisa thought the scream must have come from her lips, but she couldn't be sure. Blind with fear, she scrambled to get up, her heel catching in the hem of her dress. On her hands and knees, fighting to rise, to save Fred, she watched the man sitting so high above her. His dark-bearded face spoke of cruelty, although his voice was the whining, sneering voice of a coward.

All she could think of was the need to reach him before he could harm Fred, but nothing seemed to be working. Her body felt paralyzed . . . her legs wouldn't get untangled . . . she had to stop him. . . .

Her eyes never left the man's face, willing him to go away and leave them alone. Without another word, he raised the rifle and sighted it, his mouth twisted in a cruel smile.

"Run, Louisa!" Fred cried.

Louisa saw the flash from the gun as she heard the shot, like the roar of a cannon. She saw Fred's body lifted off the ground, then slammed downward at the impact of the bullet.

"*Fred!!*" she screamed.

The rider approached, checking to see if his bullet had done its job. He nodded in satisfaction.

Louisa looked up at the man, so high above her, on his horse, his rifle dangling from his right hand. He was still smiling, that cruel, twisted smile.

"*You've killed him!*" she shouted, her voice harsh and rasping. "*You've killed my brother, you . . . you devil!*"

Suddenly she could get up. Her body went into furious action as she leapt at the horseman and pounded on his legs and on the side of his horse, screaming, screaming.

"Wall, little missy," the horseman said when Louisa stopped to catch her breath, "you better be glad I'm a gent. I don't much cotton to folks beatin' on my horse.

Usually I shoot 'em. But I'll make an exception for you, this once."

With the butt of his gun he smashed Louisa across the side of her face, sending her flying into a heap several feet away. He rode over and looked down on her.

"Your brother chose the wrong side to be on. If you're smart, you'll tell your kinfolk they'd better see the light. This h'yere is Confederate country, with no room for Yankee lovers."

As Louisa struggled to stay conscious, he reached into his saddlebag and drew out a bundle. He tossed it at her feet.

"H'yere, Missy, I'll give you a present . . . for your brother there. It's a Yankee uniform I took off'n a dead so'jur. Bury your Yankee-lovin' brother in it, my compliments and compliments of Colonel Duff!"

He jerked the reins of his horse, and, before Louisa could grasp what he had said, he was gone, through the mesquite grove and down the hill, out of sight.

Tasting the saltiness she knew was blood from the renegade's blow, Louisa dragged herself over to where Fred lay, so still. Sobbing now, her tears blinding her, she lay beside him and cradled his head in her arms, the blood from her face running down Fred's body, mixing with his.

I should have seen him coming . . . I should have saved Fred . . . I should have. . . .

Like a heavy winter quilt, the blackness covered her.

After it was all over, Louisa tried to think back and remember what had happened that awful day. She remembered the rider, with eyes as cold as winter, raising his rifle and sighting it. Then the blast and Fred's body flung back as though it were a rag doll Emmy might throw down in a moment of anger.

Louisa's mind refused to see Fred again, all bloody and still. She could not bear to remember the moment she knew that he was dead. But how well she recalled her own actions, her screams and her fists beating on the renegade's legs and horse. His massive rifle swung towards her, smashing into the side of her face and, then, thankfully, everything went black.

From there on she had to rely on the memories of others as to what had happened. For days Papa sat by her bedside as she struggled to come out of the blackness, out of the pain, her head swathed in bandages. In his quiet, soothing voice, sometimes cracking with emotion, Papa told her about Helmut's coming upon the scene, thinking for an awful moment that both she and Fred were dead.

"He took your pulse and felt a faint heartbeat, danke Gott, but when he examined Fred's body . . . it was too late. . . ." Here Papa could not go on and Louisa felt a swelling in her throat.

"I should have heard the rider," she gasped, sobbing now. "Oh, Papa, it is my fault that Fred is dead. I was on watch . . . but I didn't hear . . . I was thinking of . . . something else . . . my fault . . . my fault. . . ."

"Nein, my dearest Louisa, you could not have done anything. Don't blame yourself. Fred would never want you to do that. Come, come, do not cry. You are upsetting your old papa, ja?"

Papa's hand gently smoothed her hair as he talked. Louisa felt some of her anguish fade under the soft sounds of Papa's voice. She lay back on her pillow and sighed, a broken, painful sigh.

Silently, Papa left her and walked out of the room.

Even when the physical pain subsided as the days and weeks passed, sorrow still held Louisa in its grip. Her aching pain at Fred's loss, as severe as the pounding in her head, returned again and again to make her weak with sadness.

Perhaps if I had been able to go to Fred's funeral, she thought, I could put my sorrow behind me. But, instead, she found herself looking up when the kitchen door opened, expecting to see his smiling face; she watched for him to come down the hillside from tending the goats as she sat in Papa's rocker on the front porch.

Then, lost in thoughts of regret, she dozed in the low, late afternoon sunlight.

She awoke with a start. A horse had knickered nearby . . . the rider again? Her heart constricted, and she sat bolt upright, her eyes trying to focus. Had he come back to kill all of them too?

"Louisa! You look frightened to death! Surely I'm not that bad looking!"

Helmut! Of course. He had come, faithfully, every day since . . . since that day when he had brought her down the hillside . . . when he had brought Fred's body home. How much he does for us even now, she thought. He checks on the goats and brings extra firewood down from the hill for Tina. He jokes and talks with Papa, rousing him from his sadness. Dear Helmut! He plays dolls with Emmy and tag with the boys. Most of all, Louisa thought, he holds my hand and keeps me in one piece when I feel I'm being torn to shreds by grief and pain.

"Ach, Louisa," he called as his horse brought him up to the porch, "is that all the greeting you have for me? Not even a 'Hello, Helmut, how are you this evening?' Nein?"

Louisa laughed, a pain shooting through her temple as she did.

"Helmut, of course I am glad to see you! Am I not always? Whatever would we have done these past few weeks without your help . . . and friendship? Come, sit down beside me and tell me all the town gossip."

"Ja, Louisa," Helmut said as he threw the reins over the porch rail and slid down from his horse. "There is much to tell tonight. I hurried out to give you the news as soon as I heard it."

Louisa, never patient when Helmut took the long way round to get to a point, exploded with exasperation.

"Tell me, tell me," she said. "Don't make me sit here wondering what you are going to say. Is the war over? What has happened?"

"Nein, my little Louisa, the war is not over. So much I wish it were so," Helmut answered with a smile at Louisa's impatience. "But, it is news of Will, Louisa . . . ."

"Will! Is he dead? Papa will not live through it if he is. Oh, Helmut, what is it?"

She grasped Helmut's arm and squeezed so hard he winced. Gently he removed her hand and rubbed his arm as he started to speak.

"Ja, let me say it, before my arm is useless to me! A man in Confederate uniform — what there was left of it — rode into town today and tied up at the Nimitz Hotel. It was not long before everyone knew his story. You know how news travels in Fredericksburg . . . ."

"Oh, for heaven's sake, Helmut, tell me . . . what do you hear of Will? Can't you hurry your story a bit?" Louisa was beside herself with anxiety.

"I apologize, Louisa, it is my nature to make a story last longer than it should. It's just that I . . ."

"Helmut!" Louisa cried out. "Please!"

"Ja, ja, you are right," Helmut said. "The man's name is Hans Ulrich. He is from north of here. He fought with the Confederacy at Shiloh and the first battle of Corinth, where he was wounded. Although he lost much blood, he survived and was later taken to a prison where he has been ever since."

"But, Will, Helmut . . . ." Louisa could not help interrupting Helmut's round-about story.

"I come to that, Louisa, in just a moment. Hans Ulrich has been paroled from the prison where he has been for so many months and allowed to come home."

"Paroled? What does that mean? And what does it have to do with Will?" Louisa asked, her hands clenched tightly to the arms of the chair. If Helmut didn't soon get to the point she thought she would burst!

"Each side, North and South, releases a certain number of prisoners at the same time, with the agreement they will no longer join in the fighting. They try to choose those whose battle wounds would not let them go back to war anyway. Hans Ulrich was one of those paroled from the Yankee prison at Corinth."

"And?" Louisa prodded.

"And Will is in that prison, Louisa! He is alive and Herr Ulrich says his condition is not too bad. He had been ill for a long time but seems to be recovering now." Helmut, looking proud of himself to have brought such good news, stood back and watched Louisa's face.

"Oh, Helmut, thank you, thank you for those good words!" Louisa pushed herself out of the rocker and gave Helmut an enthusiastic hug and a quick kiss on the cheek. Helmut, surprised, turned beet red.

"Ach, Louisa," he said when he recovered from the shock of Louisa's reaction, "I wish I could bring you good news every day, nein?"

"Tell me more, Helmut," Louisa said as she gingerly lowered herself back into the rocker, her head pounding. "Is there a chance that Will may get one of these 'paroles' any time soon? Oh, won't Papa and Tina be happy? Let's go inside and tell them."

What rejoicing followed the telling of the good news about Will! Everyone in the family talked at once, plying Helmut with questions he couldn't answer, making plans for when Will could come home, telling each other they had always known Will would be all right.

Tears of relief streamed down Papa's face. He had thought that both of his sons were lost to him. Now, at least, he knew that Will was alive and probably safe until the end of the war.

"Helmut," Papa said when he regained control of his emotions, "you have been a real friend of the von Scholl family. However can we thank you enough? Especially, for bringing us this welcome and happy news?"

"Ach, Herr von Scholl," Helmut said, ducking his head as he always did when embarrassed, "I, too, am happy that Will is safe. Although I have never met him, Louisa has told me of her older brother. I hope he can return home safely when the war is over."

Louisa took Helmut by the hand and led him out to the porch. It was that time of day, between daylight and dusk, when everything takes on a faint pink glow. Louisa sniffed the air. Yes, autumn was definitely here, although the temperatures were still mild and the mesquite trees still clung to their small, gray-green leaves.

"Do you have something else to tell me, Helmut?" she asked, as they sat on the porch steps, gazing out at the beauty before them. "I sense you are not finished telling me the news. Am I right?"

"How wise you are, for such a young person, Louisa," Helmut said with a smile and a shake of his head. "How could you have known? Ja, I do have some other news . . ."

"Before you start," Louisa interrupted, "please, please get on with it this time. Don't make me wait forever to find out what you have to say! All right?"

"Ja, it is all right, Louisa," Helmut said with a smile for her impatience. "The news is of me, personally. My uncle, as you know, is a fine carpenter, a cabinetmaker. He was well-known in the old country. He has made some very beautiful pieces, wardrobes, chests, dressers. . . ."

"There you go again, Helmut!"

"Ja, ja, I am sorry. I cannot seem to get all the words out fast enough.

"My Uncle Hermann has asked me to take a wagonload of his furniture down to the Mexican border, to Matamoras, to sell to the British or French whose merchant ships stand off the shores, ready to receive anything that can be smuggled past the Yankee blockade."

"Yes, I know. Fred was going to make a trip down there with our mohair. But then. . . ."

"I will take your mohair with me, on the wagon with Uncle's furniture. You will get a good price for it, I know, Louisa. And the British and French pay in gold, not in Confederate paper."

"Oh, that would be *wunderbar*, Helmut!" Louisa thought of how much the money would mean to Tina, even though there was not much to buy these days, even with gold. "I hope it will not be too dangerous for you to go to Mexico. Will you promise to be careful? And, oh, how I shall miss you!"

Helmut ducked his head at Louisa's words. "I shall be most careful to avoid Duff's Raiders or any of the troops who might be looking for Germans. I . . . uh . . . I shall miss you, too, Louisa."

Helmut took Louisa's hand and held it for a moment, then, releasing it, he made a little, stiff bow and backed down the steps. He untied his horse and mounted it.

"I will come for the mohair tomorrow, so that it can be packed around the furniture and then I will be on my way. Good night, Louisa. I am . . . happy . . . about your brother, Will."

"Yes, he is alive, thank God, but I hate to think of him in that prison. They say the Yankee prisons are fearful! But thank you, again, for everything, Helmut."

Louisa watched Helmut disappear into the dusk as though in a dream. Sending the mohair from his precious goats was the last gift she could give to Fred. If only she could do something for Will, to let him know she didn't mean what she said in that letter!

An idea was taking form in her head, and she sat very still so as not to disturb it. The idea was so nebulous, so timid, she had to wait patiently for it to develop.

Finally, it was there, full-blown. Of course, it was the only thing to do. And it would work. She knew exactly how. She wouldn't tell Papa and Tina until later, but now she must hurry and get everything ready. She didn't have much time. She wished it were morning so that she could get busy, but now she must try to get some sleep. Little chance for that!

By dawn Louisa had worked herself into such a state of excitement that she feared she would give her plan away to Tina or Papa as soon as they woke up. She crept into her clothes and gathered some things together and left the house. In the near-darkness she groped her way up the hill to the cave where the mohair was hidden —the cave which had hidden Fred so many times.

Feeling her way to the back of the pitch-black cave, Louisa found the stack of mohair bundles just as they'd left them. Getting gold for this precious goat's hair would be wonderful for the family . . . and for her plan. She felt around in the darkness until she found the bundle she was hunting.

She took it back to the house and sat in the rocker on the porch, waiting for the sun to break through the low-hanging clouds and for the family to arise.

In her mind she practiced the arguments she would use over Papa's and Tina's objections. She knew exactly what they would say, so she must be ready with just the right words to convince them.

I'll do it, anyway, she thought with a determination that surprised her, but I'd rather have their blessing!

Chapter Ten

"Good morning, my daughter," Papa said as he appeared in the doorway, a smile on his face. How good it was to see him happy again . . . or as happy as any of them could be with Fred gone to them forever. But Will . . . at last they knew he was alive and, hopefully, well.

"Yes, Papa," Louisa answered, matching his smile with one of her own. "It is a good morning. Where is Tina? Is she not up yet?"

"Oh, ja, she has been up, sitting at the table, for a while now. She writes a letter to Melissa, who perhaps has not heard the good news about Will. I only hope the letter will get through . . . so many are being lost these days."

"Yes," Louisa said, "I had almost forgotten Melissa. She will be so happy to know her husband is safe.

"But I must interrupt Tina in her letter writing. I need to talk to you both, before the twins and Emmy awake."

"Oh, is it something so important, Louisa, it cannot wait for Tina to finish her letter?" Papa sat down on the top step and leaned against the hand rail. This was his usual place to sit since Louisa had taken over the rocking chair as she got better. Now she jumped up, with just the slightest twinge of pain, and offered Papa his rocking chair.

"Here, Papa, sit here. You may have your chair back. As of this moment, I am all well! And when I tell you my news you will be so excited, you will need the feel of your chair beneath you, I promise!"

Louisa could contain herself no longer. She went into the house and took Tina by the hand.

"Come with me, Tina, I have very important things to tell you and they cannot wait. You can finish your letter to Melissa later."

Amidst grumbling and complaining from Tina, the two sisters went outside and joined Papa on the porch.

"All right, little sister, what can be so important that you interrupt me when I'm writing such good news to our sister-in-law?" Tina's curiosity got the better of her irritation.

Now that she had them there, Louisa lost some of her courage. All night she had rehearsed what she would say, but now she hesitated. She took a deep breath and began.

"Helmut told me last night that he is leaving today for Mexico with a load of his uncle's furniture. He has offered to take our mohair and sell it to the British or French for us."

"How wonderful!" Tina exclaimed. "How we will ever repay that young man for all his kindnesses I do not know. Be sure to thank him for us, Louisa, when he comes to get the mohair. And wish him Godspeed!"

Tina turned to go back to her letter writing, but Louisa took her hand and held it.

"There's more, Tina. Promise you'll listen to every word I say and not rush in with arguments. Promise?"

"Of couse, Louisa, what a silly thing to make me promise!"

"Tell us, Louisa, what has you so excited?" Papa said, reading his daughter's face and actions.

"It is hard to start, but I am getting as bad as Helmut at not being able to get my words out.

"I have a plan. You may not like it, but it is very important to me that I do this, so please, please hear me out!"

"Louisa, you are trying my patience! What kind of a plan do you have? I cannot imagine what you can be talking about," Tina said, exasperation in her voice.

"All right, here it is," Louisa said, looking first at Papa and then back at Tina. "I am going with Helmut, to take the mohair to Mexico and get our gold for it. . . ."

"*What?*" Tina cried. "You know you cannot do that! It would be very dangerous, not only for you, but for Helmut, to take you along!"

"Tina, you promised. Please. Hear me out.

"I plan to dress in Fred's old clothes — they should fit me fairly well. I will cut my hair and wear one of Helmut's German caps on my head. I will be his cousin, along to help unload the freight."

"But . . . but. . . ." Tina sputtered. Papa sat very still, in stunned silence.

"Now listen to the rest, please," Louisa went on.

"When we get to Matamoras I will find a ship to take me to New Orleans. While on the ship I will put on this old Union uniform that devil of Duff's left behind. I will pretend to be an orderly and get into a hospital unit. From there I will make my way to Corinth, Mississippi, to the prison where the Yankees are holding Will.

"Somehow I will figure a way for Will to escape from the prison . . . and I will bring him home to you, Papa! Isn't it a glorious plan?"

An hour later the argument still raged. Papa in his quiet way tried to persuade Louisa that it was too dangerous. Tina cried and wrung her hands.

"Are you trying to get yourself killed?" she cried. "Mama is probably turning over in her grave this very instant! She wanted you to be a lady . . . and what do you want? To cut your beautiful hair . . . and be a . . . a . . . boy!"

"No, Tina," Louisa said, beginning to lose patience. "A soldier! That is what I'll be. Maybe I can even do some

87

good . . . tending the wounded and sick. Many women have done the same in this war. Papa has read me stories in his newspaper about them and all the good work they are doing for the men in battle."

"But you're too young!" Tina said, for the fortieth time.

"In a month I'll be sixteen! Not too young at all."

But Tina would not give up. "Louisa," she said, "think of the risk you are taking! You could get killed!"

Louisa smiled. "What about when I was a baby, Tina? Did you think of the risks you took when you rode into that Indian camp to rescue me from the chief and his old squaw? I think you were just about my age then." Louisa saw Tina's face flush. "Fred said one time that your rescuing me was probably the most exciting thing that ever happened to you. Tell me, Tina, would you have done it differently? Are you sorry you risked your life to save me?"

Tina's lips became a tight, straight line, as though they had been drawn on a chalkboard with a ruler, Louisa thought. Without looking directly at her sister, Tina spoke with a tightness in her voice which matched her lips.

"That was entirely different. I see no comparison. I won't agree to this foolish plan that might see you hurt or killed without a hope of success in rescuing Will.

"That is all I have to say on the subject! Now, I have a letter to finish."

Tina turned away from Louisa and marched, back stiff and straight, into the house.

Louisa turned to her father for support and understanding. She must convince him that what she wanted to do was right and that it would work.

"Papa?" she said, her voice small and tentative. "You do believe me and see what I must do for you . . . and for Will, don't you?"

"Ja, my dear daughter, I see it all. Your courage and your love, for your family. But, I am afraid. I cannot let you do this. I cannot give my permission for you to do this thing. Nein. You must not go."

"*Papa!*" Louisa could not believe her ears. She had been so sure that she could convince, if not Tina, who tended to be stubborn sometimes, but certainly Papa, who almost always gave in to her pleading.

Shaking his head, Papa got up from the rocking chair and walked slowly into the house, leaving Louisa stunned. How could this have happened? What would she do now? How could she give up her plan to rescue Will? But, then, how could she disobey Papa? She had never disobeyed him in her life!

Flopping into the rocking chair which was still moving from Papa leaving it, she gave in to the tears which had been fighting to stream down her cheeks for some minutes now.

How long she sat in the chair she didn't know. Sometime midmorning she left the porch and took the path up the hill to Fred's cave. Her cheeks felt stiff with dried tears, her throat ached from her sobs. Now she felt a deep sadness inside, as though she were lost in the woods but no one would help her find the way out.

For hours she sat in the cave, thinking of Fred, of Will, of Papa and Tina. It was nearly dark when she made her way slowly down the hillside and into the house. Everyone was seated at the table, eating. Papa motioned for Louisa to take her seat, a small, sad smile on his face. He must have warned the family to leave her alone with her thoughts, because no one spoke a word to her.

After the supper dishes were cleared away, Louisa sat once more on the porch, silent and far away.

Finally it was bed time. Louisa shivered as she crawled between the sheets.

Tina put out the lamp and the house was still. For a long time Louisa lay motionless, her body tense, until she was sure everyone was asleep. Then she sat up on the edge of the bed and gingerly lowered her feet onto the cold floor.

She knew what she had to do.

Creeping silently through the house, she felt along the wall until she located the table where Tina had been writing the letter to Melissa. The moonlight, filtered through the shutters covering the small windows, was little help. She could hear gentle breathing from the room where the twins and Emily slept; Papa's snoring was not so gentle. He always snored the loudest when he went to bed in an unhappy mood. Louisa shook her head in sadness, thinking of Papa and the grief she was going to cause him.

She found the table and felt around on it until she found Tina's small store of paper and the pencil. She went back the way she had come, careful to make no sound opening the door. Once again on the porch, she sat down on the top step and thought what she wanted to say in her note to the family.

The full moon silvered the porch, the yard and the trees beyond. At the edge of the trees a young deer stood, warily watching her. Its ears and back were silver too. Louisa barely noticed the deer or the beautiful night; her mind was too full. She was, though, grateful for the light.

"*Dearest ones,*" she wrote, her mouth twisted in total concentration. "*I am so sorry for what I have to do, because I know how all of you will worry about me. But I must go to find Will. I love you. Louisa.*"

She had no idea how she would rescue Will; she only knew that she had to go. Somehow, tomorrow, after Helmut had packed up the mohair and left, she would follow and catch up with him. Papa would be unhappy with her, but maybe he would eventually come to understand and forgive her disobedience.

She gave a guilty start as she heard a sound behind her. Quickly putting the note under her skirt, she looked around. Tina stood, silently looking at the moon, then sighed and turned toward her younger sister.

"I couldn't sleep, either," she said, so softly Louisa could barely make out the words.

"I've been thinking about what you said, about when I went after you and faced the Indians alone, the way you plan to face the soldiers, to rescue Will. You were right and I was wrong . . . it is the same. I just didn't want to think so.

"I . . . uh . . . I have changed my mind. I think that you must go and try to rescue Will and bring him home to Papa." Tina stood, waiting for Louisa to say something.

Louisa's heart was so full, of love for her sister and of joy that they had finally come to an understanding, that she could not move for a moment. Then, rushing to Tina, she threw her arms around her and kissed her on the cheek.

"Oh, Tina, I love you. Thank you for understanding . . . and for having the courage to say that you were wrong. I know how hard that was for you."

"Yes," Tina said, with a small laugh. "I do tend to be bossy and stubborn, don't I? It is just my way and I cannot help it. But I do understand and want you to go to Will with my blessing. Of course, I'm not speaking for Papa. I'm afraid he will be very upset, but I'll handle him, don't worry."

"Thank you, Tina," Louisa said, her voice shaking with emotion. "Wait here while I get something in the house. There is one other thing I want you to do for me."

Leaving Tina wondering what she meant, Louisa crept silently around the big, dark room until she located Tina's sewing table. From the small drawer she withdrew the scissors which had been Mama's many years ago.

As she stepped back onto the porch she held the scissors out to Tina.

"Here," she said, "chop off this hair for me. You will do a much neater job than I could."

Tina took the scissors, looked at Louisa's long, fair hair, silver in the moonlight, and shuddered.

"I hate to think what Mama would say!" she said, holding a large strand of Louisa's hair in her left hand, the scissors poised in her right.

Snip!

Louisa felt a shock go through her. She hadn't realized until that moment that she was really going to put her daring plan into action. Could she do it? Could she fool the authorities into thinking she was a man—and a soldier at that?

Snip!

Long hanks of pale flaxen hair fell to the porch floor.

"It is done," Tina whispered. "I cannot bear to look at you — your beautiful hair cropped as short as any soldier's.

"Ach, I've just thought of something. What will we tell Papa in the morning? How will we explain your hair?"

Tina looked as though she would like to gather up all the strands of hair on the porch floor and somehow fasten them back on Louisa's head, rather than try to explain to Papa what they had done.

"Stop worrying so much, Tina," Louisa said with a smile at her older sister's confusion. "I will wrap my head in a towel and tell Papa that I have just washed my hair. He will not question that. After I have gone, ask him to forgive me for lying to him . . . and for disobeying him. I hope he will."

"He will," Tina said. "Maybe not at once, but after the shock of it all wears off, I think he'll understand that you had to go and that I had to help you. He'll forgive us both, I hope."

The sisters embraced and held each other tightly for a moment. Then Tina broke away.

"Come, let us see if we can get some sleep for the rest of this short night. It will be dawn much too soon."

In the distance a coyote called to his partner who answered. The second coyote was not far into the stand of trees where the deer had stood. He did not call again.

Hand in hand, Louisa and Tina left the moonlight and went into the darkness of the house. Louisa crawled into her bed and lay quietly, thinking how good it was that she and Tina were friends again. It would make the difficult trip she was facing much easier to bear, knowing she had her sister's blessing.

She slept soundly for the rest of the night.

Morning came much too early for Louisa. She stretched and yawned and ran her fingers through her hair, as she always did right after awakening.

Ach! Her hair! For a moment she had forgotten that her hair was shorn, like one of the Angora goats! She grabbed a towel and wound it around her head. As she dressed she hoped Papa would believe her story and not suspect what she planned to do.

"Someone's coming! I hear the horses," Sam yelled from outside.

Louisa went to the window. "It's Helmut, and he has someone with him! I expected him to come alone." She raced outside and stood on the top step of the porch, waiting for the wagon to reach the yard.

"It's Hermann Schultz, Helmut's uncle. He must be here to help load the mohair." With relief, Louisa noticed the saddled horse tied behind the wagon. Herr Schultz was not planning to go with Helmut, thank goodness!

Everyone crowded onto the porch as the wagon, loaded with furniture, approached. Papa walked out to meet Herr Schultz, while Helmut started toward the house.

"Good morning, Helmut," Louisa said, smiling, as she hurried to join Helmut. "Why don't we go for a short walk while Papa and your uncle have a chat. Already I hear Papa telling Herr Schultz about our early days in

Industry. That story takes some time in the telling . . . at least when Papa tells it."

The two strolled away from the others and from the house. Louisa fought for the courage to tell Helmut her plan to join him. When she did tell him, it took several repeatings to convince him she was serious.

"Well, Louisa," he said, finally, "if you are determined to do this foolish thing, of course I will help you. But it is very dangerous!"

"I know, Helmut, but I have to do it. Now, go help the others bring the mohair down from the cave, but not a word of what I plan to do. Papa is not to know until after I've gone. I'll find some excuse to follow you, as though I intend to return."

"Ja, Louisa, I understand, and I will keep your secret," Helmut said, with a curious glance at Louisa's head swathed in the big towel but too polite to ask questions. Instead he hurried back to the house to gather up his helpers and get about the business of loading the mohair.

Several hours later the men and boys had lashed the mohair bundles between the pieces of furniture and to the sides of the wagon, so that the goats' wool protected the fine woodwork that Herr Schultz had so lovingly produced. He had said his farewells to Helmut and the others and had ridden his horse back to town, unaware of the little drama that was about to take place.

With a wave to Papa and the others and a small smile for Tina, Helmut climbed up onto the big wagon and clicked an order to the horses. Straining against the heavy load they moved slowly, then a little faster, heading toward the road that would take them to the Mexican border.

Louisa watched, wondering how she could join Helmut without Papa suspecting anything. She believed she knew what might work.

She ran into the house and pulled her bedroll, tied tight and holding the few belongings she could take with her, out of her dresser drawer. She shoved Fred's trousers and his old blue chambray shirt, along with the bundle which had been under her bed, deep inside the bedroll. Then she lowered it out of the window, and it dropped silently onto the ground.

She went out onto the porch and put her arm around Tina's waist. "Goodbye, Tina," she whispered, taking care that Papa was not watching them from the yard where he stood talking to the twins and Emmy. "Take good care of Papa and the young ones, will you? I hope to see you soon with Will riding beside me!"

Louisa went down the steps of the porch and strolled around the yard, trying to look casual. As she came to the corner of the house, near where the wagon had stood, she cried out.

"Oh, look, Helmut's bedroll! It must have fallen off the wagon while they were packing the mohair! He will be lost without his clothes and other things. What a shame!"

Tina understood immediately what Louisa was doing and called out to her, "Why don't you saddle up Buster and ride after him? He can't be too far away by now."

"That's a good idea, daughter," Papa said, smiling at Tina. "It will give Louisa and Helmut a chance to say their personal goodbyes, ja?" Louisa thought she spied a twinkle in Papa's eyes as he had his little joke.

Her stomach churned as she thought how easy it had been and how unhappy it made her to fool Papa this way. He hadn't even noticed the towel around her head, after all. She ran to the barn and threw a saddle on Buster. She knew that, after she left with Helmut, the old horse would find his way home easily enough; he loved his stall and his dinner.

She fastened the bedroll behind her saddle and climbed up onto Buster's back.

"Well, here I go," she said to all of them, standing around her and watching, each thinking different thoughts. Tina looked worried; Papa, serene and the twins, envious.

95

"Be careful," Papa said.

"Hurry back," Zach called.

Tina ran up to Louisa, pretending to adjust the strap holding the bedroll.

"Take care, Louisa," she whispered, her voice quavering.

"I shall," Louisa replied, tears perilously close. "Remember, as soon as I get deep enough into the woods, I will change into Fred's old clothes and take this silly towel off of my head. From then on I no longer will be Louisa Emily von Scholl, but, I will be known as Louis Emil Robinson. I'll write as often as I can. Goodbye, dear Tina."

Tina looked as though she could not breathe.

"Goodbye," she whispered, her eyes full of tears. "Goodbye, Louis Emil Robinson."

Part Two
Louis Emil Robinson

Chapter Eleven

Baton Rouge, Louisiana
December 25, 1862

The hospital smelled of blood, rotten food and death;
rows of cots held them, the boys who had given up limbs
and lives to the cause of the Union.

Louisa held her breath for a moment as she always
did when she entered this huge room full of suffering. It
wasn't just the stench, which was bad enough; it was the
feel of the place, the hopelessness, the fear, the pain.

Merry Christmas! Louisa thought.

Not too merry for most of these young men. So far
this week Louisa, in her role of Orderly Louis Emil Robinson,
had assisted at four amputations and sent five soldiers to
the dead-house. She still shuddered to think of what they
went through, with little or no anesthetics to ease their
pain. Chloroform and ether were both scarce; a tumbler
full of whiskey often was all they had. How many bullets
had teeth marks in them, as the boy from Ohio or Illinois
bit down to keep from screaming!

She started on her rounds, stopping at each cot, speaking
to the soldier lying there, bathing him and giving him a
drink, wishing him a Merry Christmas. How little the
doctors let the orderlies do for the patients! If the sur-
geons weren't so jealous of their power, the orderlies, like
she and the young men in her company, could administer

much more aid to the patients than they now were allowed to. She had heard of women nurses, under the formidable Dorothea Dix, who kept the areas around the hospital tents cleaned up, who insisted on better cleanliness inside, and who tried to persuade the doctors to use more sanitary means of working with their patients.

Usually the nurses were berated for their suggestions. Some day people would look back and realize what a lot of good the women had done in this war . . . maybe! Right now, the doctors made it clear they didn't need or want the women around. It was enough for them to read to the wounded, or carry letters to their kin or cut a lock of a dying boy's hair and deliver it to his grieving mother. But stay out of the operating room!

"*Froliche Weihnachten*," Louisa whispered to the German boy from Pennsylvania. "Merry Christmas." How few German words I know, and how I regret not learning more about my heritage from Papa and Tina.

She had been in this hospital, posing as Private Louis Emil Robinson, for about a week, since the Yankees under Major General Banks had moved into Baton Rouge, hoping soon to capture Vicksburg and make the entire Mississippi River theirs. But the Confederates didn't abandon Vicksburg for the taking, as they had Baton Rouge, where they left the Yankees as little as possible, burning hundreds of bales of cotton, sinking boats that couldn't make it past the fleet of Admiral David G. Farragut.

No, the Yanks would have to battle for Vicksburg; rebel guns were poised on top of the high clay embankments, rebel soldiers had dug into trenches in the town. According to what Louisa overheard the doctors saying, the town of Vicksburg was in for a long, painful siege, as northern gunboats, mortar boats and rams filled the river just out of rebel gun range. President Lincoln had instructed his General Ulysses S. Grant to take the city by any means. The newest rumor was that a canal would be built to divert the Mississippi away from Vicksburg, making its big guns atop the cliff useless. What a job that would be, Louisa thought. I wonder if it will work.

Still, she sighed, I'm no closer to finding Will than when I left Fredericksburg. I promised Papa I'd have Will home by Christmas. Everything takes so long! First the trip with Helmut to Matamoras took at least a week longer than planned; rain slowed them down and twice they lost their way. Then the business of selling the mohair and getting the gold from the British ship captain, arranging for her passage on his ship, and the tearful farewell with Helmut, promising she'd see him by Christmas. But, instead, she was here in this wretched hospital, knowing no one, on Christmas day. How alone she felt!

I reckon Christmas makes everyone think of home and family, she thought . . . everyone who is away, that is. I miss them so.

She wondered what Tina was baking in the oven today. Had they found any meat for the Christmas feast? Her own Christmas "feast" had consisted of a piece of fatty pork, some hard tack and coffee.

She thought of Helmut. What was he doing today? Was he thinking of her and wondering where and how she was? She hoped so. He had been so upset at the thought of her leaving on the British ship for New Orleans that he had decided to go along. . . . Louisa would not hear of it.

"I need you to take the gold back to my family and to look after them. They need you more than I do, Helmut!" she had said. Hurt, he had said goodbye and left for town to take the wagon home. He had not looked back.

She had wanted to run after him, to kiss him goodbye, to hear his voice wish her well. But she couldn't. After all, she was now a Union soldier in uniform, "ready to return to duty, paroled after having been captured and held prisoner by the Rebs," according to the forged papers bought

101

with one of her precious gold coins. Tearfully, she had watched Helmut until he disappeared from view.

Surprisingly, no one had questioned her, no one had guessed she was not what she pretended to be. On the long trip to Mexico she had practiced lowering her voice a few notes and walking with a longer stride.

When she had taken the Yankee uniform out of its hiding place and shaken it out, she nearly abandoned the whole plan. The dirty, wrinkled uniform stunk from old sweat, blood and heavens-knew-what; the bullet hole in the lower chest made her shudder to think of the young man who had worn this coat last. She brushed the wool as hard as she could with her hair brush, dust and bugs flying everywhere. With the sewing kit she had brought from home, she mended the bullet hole and sewed the few gold coins she had kept from the mohair sale into the lining of the jacket. Then, drawing a deep breath of distaste, she put it on, rolling Fred's old clothes into a bundle to be saved in case she needed to get out of uniform sometime. It very nearly fit; for once she was thankful for her height. She pulled the belt in a couple of notches and hiked up the trousers about an inch. Not too bad.

So far she had gotten away with her deception. She just must make sure not to get sick or wounded. A doctor's examination would put an end to her plan to rescue Will. And she didn't even know for sure where he was yet.

"Over here, orderly!" The voice belonged to Major Johnston, not one of Louisa's favorites.

"Yes, sir," she said and regretfully left her "boys" to see what old "Tight Lips" wanted. She had nicknamed all the doctors and officers, to keep her sense of humor intact. There was "Fat Cheek" Dr. Blackstone, who always had a wad of tobacco in his mouth. And "Fur Face" Dr. Edmonds, whose beard and facial hair obscured all but his burning black eyes.

Dr. Johnston had earned "Tight Lips" because he never opened his mouth when he talked, his upper and lower teeth seemed to be fastened together. She had never seen him smile, although she had to admit there wasn't much to smile about in this place.

"Here's another one to haul to the dead-house," he said between his teeth. "Get it out of here so we can have this cot for the next one."

Louisa looked under the bloody sheet at the body of the dead soldier. So young! He couldn't have been more than fourteen! She swallowed hard and covered his face again. Pushing the heavy cart across the rough field to the dead-house was a chore, but she liked to think it was the last thing she could do for a boy who'd given up the most precious thing, his life, for his country.

The dead-house was no more than a shack, off to the side of the other buildings, where the bodies were deposited each day, to be collected for burial the following morning.

The corpses were laid out in rows on a shelf. Soldiers would even now be digging another trench, six feet wide and two feet deep. The bodies would be buried side by side, feet and heads touching the edges of the trench. Another crew would fill the trench with dirt and go off to other duties. No service would be held. There wasn't time. Too many sick and wounded men awaited someone's attention to give much time to the dead. Louisa said a little prayer over the young soldier's body, as she did over each one she hauled to the dead-house.

"Psst, Louis," a voice spoke in a rasping whisper.

It was Billy Yost, one of the other orderlies, one who had insisted on befriending "Louis," despite Louisa's efforts to stay aloof for fear of being found out. But Billy wouldn't take her actions as unfriendly; he had decided that Louis was just shy and needed a friend. No amount of discouragement fazed him.

"Psst, Louis," Billy said again, bringing her back to the present. "Come on out of that there fearful place and let's us amble down to the river. I h'year there's some ships covered all over with steel armor, with huge guns, headin' up river toward Vicksburg. Some says Admiral Farragut be goin' to try to run past Vicksburg's guns with his fleet. I'm mighty glad I'm not on one of them boats right now!

"Come on, I tell yer, old Johnston will never know!"

"Thanks, Billy," Louisa said, her lips twitching at Billy's terrible English. "But I've got work that has to be done by nightfall. Better not leave today. Maybe some other time, all right? You go on, and then tell me all about it."

"Wall, I guess if yer gonna shimmy up to them doctors and officers, ain't nothing I kin do about it. I'll see yer later."

Billy, stubby and with what Tina would have called a "shiftless air" about him, turned and shuffled out of the dead-house. "Billy Yank" Louisa had named him, the name all Yankee soldiers were called now, along with "Johnny Reb" for the Confederates. She would have to figure a way to discourage his friendship. She couldn't take a chance he might guess the truth.

Secretly she yearned to go to the river and see Admiral Farragut's fleet. She had come to Baton Rouge on a hospital ship headed upriver for ports above Vicksburg, but they couldn't get past those big, high-placed guns and so had to turn back to Baton Rouge. She had hoped to go as far north as the Louisiana border, then to find transportation across the state to Corinth, Mississippi, supposing Will was still there.

Was he? Or had the Yankees moved him by now? And how would she ever reach Corinth now? She'd probably be stuck here for the rest of the war and not accomplish what she had set out to do — to rescue Will.

At least I'm doing worthy work while I wait, Louisa thought, as she left the dead-house and went back to the hospital to scrub the mess hall floor. I feel that I am doing something to be proud of, not just the piddly housework things I would be doing at home. I always knew that if I were a man, I could accomplish something!

She decided to write a letter home after hours. That would be her Christmas present to all of her dear family. There was so much to tell — of her trip to Baton Rouge and her work and the wonderful, brave soldiers she attended.

She missed her family so much, especially today because it was Christmas, but even more last month on her birthday! At least on Christmas some of the orderlies and one or two doctors had wished her a happy day; on her birthday, her sixteenth, no one knew and she had no friends in New Orleans to share her day. No, it was nothing like she had always dreamed her sixteenth birthday would be. She had been very lonely and that night, in the cold, damp barracks, she had cried herself to sleep.

Well, there was nothing to do but go on and make the best of it. She certainly had things better than any of these poor sick and wounded boys!

As she reached the door of the hospital she heard the moans and cries of the suffering. More beds were filled with sick soldiers than with wounded ones. Most of the wounded were being brought to Baton Rouge from other hospitals, but the illnesses lived with the men in their tents and struck at so many that, at one time, nearly half the regiment was on sick list.

She took the patients their meager supper and wished them Merry Christmas again, feeling guilty that she could do so little for them.

Slowly, she returned to her barracks to write her Christmas letter home.

Chapter Twelve

As the months piled up, one after the other, Louisa despaired of ever reaching Corinth and Will. Her duties at the hospital kept her busy and depressed. So many fine young men sick and dying daily, with little or no help from her and the others who served with her. Helplessness ate at her being, nudging a rebellious streak which she knew was useless but kept her on edge and nervous all the time.

Why couldn't they do more for these soldiers who were dying by the hundreds, on both sides of this nasty war? Dr. Johnston assured her that as many, if not more, rebel soldiers were dying as were Yanks. She found that not at all consoling! All these young men, wasted! And for what? Her mind rejected all the pat answers she heard from the Yankee doctors; she eavesdropped on their conversations without a tinge of remorse. How else would she learn what was happening out there?

That was how, months after it happened, Louisa learned about Lincoln's Emancipation Proclamation. It had happened shortly after she had arrived in Baton Rouge, January 1st, to be exact, January 1, 1863. Lincoln wrote a paper, proclaiming all the slaves in the states at war with the Union to be free!

Louisa rejoiced at this news until she overheard old Tight Lips smirk that this "proclamation was a joke —

didn't free any slaves atall! The ones living up north are still slaves and the ones in the South will never hear about their freedom as long as their owners are in charge!"

One of the other doctors said, "Yes, there will have to be an amendment to the constitution of the United States, after this war is over, before all the slaves will be free."

"That'll never happen!" predicted Tight Lips, going off to make his rounds.

Louisa didn't know what to think. Were the slaves free or not? She put that problem aside, to be pondered later, as she heard her patients calling for their breakfast.

The siege of Vicksburg continued, month after month, as spring turned into hot, muggy summer. According to the Yankee spies, the citizens of Vicksburg were living like animals, dug into hillside caves to avoid the mortar shells and minié balls hurled at them daily. Dr. Johnston and the others rejoiced in the suffering and deprivation of the people on the bluff.

It made Louisa want to cry. Those people, especially the women and children, didn't deserve to have to fear for their lives, starving and miserable, dodging bullets and spending their last few pennies on whatever they could find for their dinner! Mule meat was dear, but it was said that a plump rat could be had for five plugs of tobacco! Louisa shuddered. Wasn't this a soldier's war? Why should the innocent townsfolk have to suffer like this?

No matter how bad it was in the city of Vicksburg, the Confederates hung on to it with a fierce tenacity that surprised General Grant and his officers. The building of the canal to bypass Vicksburg was not going well and all efforts to attack the city failed.

Old Tight Lips and his friends wagered on the chances that Grant would succeed in taking this last Confederate stronghold on the Mississippi.

In the meantime, I'm stranded here in Baton Rouge, Louisa thought, wondering if I'll ever be free to find Will.

Then on the third of July it happened. Tight Lips called her into his tent, along with Billy Yost and twelve other orderlies.

"It is necessary to get medical help up to Corinth, Mississippi," Dr. Johnston said, "as there is an epidemic of typhoid. Many of our men have already died, including about half the staff."

Louisa blinked, unbelieving. Was she actually to be sent to Corinth? The place all her heart yearned to see? What luck! She could have kissed old Tight Lips, but she doubted if he could get his lips to pucker up for a kiss! Louisa giggled, then quickly surpressed it, afraid someone would notice.

Will? Louisa thought with alarm, after the first joy of the news wore off a little. Would she get to Corinth only to find that Will, too, had died of the dreaded fever?

Dr. Johnston continued, "Admiral Farragut is willing to help us run the blockade past the Vicksburg guns so that we can send aid to our men up there. He has done it several times with success, and I have no doubt he will be successful this time too."

He lost several ships that first time, Louisa thought. Am I going to end up on the bottom of the Mississippi River?

Tight Lips continued. "You will go aboard the hospital ship *New York* at sunset. Medical supplies and food for the journey are already aboard. Two doctors, all I can spare, will accompany you. You will set sail at dawn, proceeding past Vicksburg, up the Mississippi River to Memphis and then overland to Corinth. There will be ambulance wagons and mules waiting for you when you debark the *New York*.

"After rendering any aid you can, you will return to Memphis with the sickest of the men, who will be treated at the general hospital in Memphis. On the trip up the Mississippi the *New York* will stop at several ports to pick up patients to be left at the Memphis hospital.

"Take all your belongings. This is a permanent move, and you won't be returning to Baton Rouge but will receive further orders on your return to Memphis. Good luck."

With those words Dr. Johnston turned his attention to the stack of reports on his shaky, makeshift desk.

As she made her rounds, Louisa spoke to each sick soldier and mentally bid him goodbye. She had grown fond of some of the men who had spent months in the hospital trying to get well. Some had left, thanking her for all her help; others she had sadly transported to the dead-house. Most of these unfortunate ones had died of disease — malaria, typhoid, measles, cholera and dysentery. They had never seen a battlefield.

Louisa dashed off a quick note to the family, telling them the good news of her trip to Corinth. She promised to write again as soon as she arrived there.

Packing her few possessions took very little time. She made sure that Fred's old clothes were packed tightly inside her bedroll. How she wished she could put them on — at least they were cleaner than this louse-infested uniform! Wouldn't Tina have a fit if she knew that her baby sister hadn't had a real bath since this adventure began? "Spit" baths had to do, and those only when the men were all bedded down and asleep or out on duty. So far, no one had noticed that she never used the open latrines, or "sinks" as they were called. She had to sneak off into the swampy woods and take her chances with bugs and snakes. Somehow, when she devised this plan back in Fredericksburg, she hadn't given a thought to these practical matters. It had seemed so brave and romantic! Well, she'd have some tales to tell when she got home. When she and Will got home.

The *New York*, all packed and ready, steamed out of Baton Rouge harbor as the eastern sky's first light appeared on the horizon. Captain Arbuckle, a huge, red-haired giant of a man, ordered "Cast off!" and Louisa'a heart lurched as she realized that she was truly on her way to Will, after what seemed like a lifetime of waiting.

Accompanying the little hospital ship was an iron-clad, a gun boat and Admiral Farragut's flag ship. Louisa stood on deck as the morning wore on, waiting for a glimpse of the high, clay banks of Vicksburg. The river teemed with ships of all sizes and types. Louisa's eyes widened as she realized how vulnerable they were in their little, unarmed hospital ship. The big guns atop the Vicksburg cliff could pick them off easily.

She heard voices aboard the *New York*, voices exclaiming something she couldn't make out. The crew crowded up on the front deck and all of them, in high excitement, shouted and pointed at the cliffs of Vicksburg. What could it be? She knew it was the Fourth of July; was there some sort of celebration going on? No, the folks of Vicksburg had nothing to celebrate these days. Louisa edged forward to hear what they were shouting.

"It's over, it's over!" one sailor cried, flinging his cap in the air. "Vicksburg has fallen! The whole Mississipi is ours!"

"How does he know that?" Louisa asked a quieter member of the crew who stood staring at the city, a big grin on his face.

"See the white flags all over the place, up on that there hill?" the sailor answered without looking around. "They're surrenderin' the city, fella, that's what they're doin'. Hallelujah! Praise the Lord!"

Tears welled in Louisa's eyes, and she quickly turned away so that the sailor couldn't see such "unmanly" behavior. Those poor people in Vicksburg! Maybe Grant's army would give them some food now. Maybe they'd no longer have to eat rats! Maybe they could leave their hillside caves and go home — if there were any homes left standing.

How thankful I am that my family is safe in Texas! They may have hardships but nothing like what these poor people have endured. The people of Vicksburg may be the "enemy," but I wish them the best. Surely even General Grant must admire their bravery and their stubborn will to hold on for so long!

The gunboats left the *New York* on its own. Danger from mortar shells was past, and they had more important things to do than worry about one little hospital ship.

Later, Louisa remembered the trip to Corinth with mixed feelings. She loved being aboard ship, even a creaky old hospital ship like the *New York*; loved the feel of the meandering Mississippi River rolling beneath the ship's hull; loved the green sweep of the landscape as it passed before her fascinated eyes. But then, there was the other side: the suffering of the soldiers, the hard and sometimes gruesome work she was required to do and, worse, her own fears about what she would learn when she reached Corinth and tried to locate Will.

The ship made occasional stops to pick up patients at towns along the route. They were not too gently transported to the ship and dumped aboard deck. Most were suffering from some malady, a few with typhoid.

"Ye can't put them soljurs with the typhoid down in the hold of my ship," Captain Arbuckle roared, his face almost as red as his hair. "I won't have my crew coming down with that fearsome disease, I won't!"

"But, Captain," Louisa protested, "what shall we do? These men are sick and need our help."

"Leave 'em up here on deck, then, if ye must have 'em aboard. But not below deck, y'hear? That's an order!"

"Yes, sir," Louisa said, determined to be one of those to care for the sick soldiers on the deck of the ship. At least it was warm (insufferably hot below) so that they wouldn't take a chill. The fresh air would probably be good for them.

As usual, when not working, Louisa kept herself apart from the others, fearing her secret's discovery. And also as usual, Billy Yost would not permit her to stay alone, but insisted on joining her every chance he got.

"Oi, Louis, ya be a strange feller," Billy complained. "Ya work like twenty demons, and treat them sick boys like they be your own kin. But, then, fer the rest of us, ya puts on the unfriendliest face I ever did see! Like ya didn't want none of us to take to ya. I 'fess, I jest don't unnerstand it."

"I'm sorry, Billy. I don't mean to be unfriendly. I just have a lot on my mind, my family at home, you know?" Louisa tried to sound natural, though her heart thumped rapidly any time she had to speak in her "Louis" voice.

"Sure, lad, I unnerstand," Billy said, giving her a slap on the back that almost knocked her over. "But we all has worries alike, and it be good for ya to has summon to talk to, y'see?"

"I have to go below now, Billy," Louisa said, anxious to get away. "I've ten bunks to attend to and ten patients to feed." She hurried away, leaving Billy scratching his head in puzzlement as though he just couldn't "figger that fella out."

Louisa worried as she climbed down into the smelly, dank hold of the ship. Could she keep up this masquerade in the confines of the small ship, for as long as this journey would take? She couldn't wait to arrive at Memphis and be back on shore, to get the whole trip over with and reach Corinth.

Would Will be there? Would he be all right? And how could she spirit Will away, back to Texas and home? Questions seethed through her mind as she made up beds with dirty sheets and fed patients cold gruel for breakfast.

Chapter Thirteen

Louisa lost track of time on the trip up the Mississippi River to Memphis. It seemed to last forever. Then they were there, getting the patients off the ship and into the big hospital, packing themselves and their belongings into the waiting wagons which would take them to the train station for the overland journey to Corinth. Louisa was surprised at the change in orders; she had expected that they would go from Memphis to Corinth by wagon. But, instead, they would travel the Memphis & Little Rock Railroad, just as though there were no war and they were on a trip for pleasure!

"I thought the rebels always blew up all the railroad tracks or somehow destroyed them as they retreated from a place," Louisa said.

Billy Yost explained. "Way back last December, Grant pulled some of his troops from the Tallahatchie, with orders ter reopen and guard the railroad between Memphis and Corinth. That secesh bunch ain't had a chance ter blow up a train er pull up a rail since then."

She had had no chance to see what Memphis looked like, except to note its bustling harbor. She wished she could have had time to explore the city. But it was without regret that she boarded the train for the trip overland: they were on their way to Corinth — and Will.

Louisa had never been on a steam train before; her eyes grew wide as she heard the giant iron monster let out a sigh and then, with a mighty heave, start down the tracks, its shrill whistle blowing. As they chugged along she pressed her face against the glass and watched the scenery whiz by. She had never moved so swiftly in her life. It was magic!

She spent her time daydreaming about Will and how surprised he'd be to see her, and how she could get him away from there and home to Papa and Tina.

She made up little scenes in her mind: Will might be sick, but she, Louisa, would cure him and smuggle him out of the prison on a moonless night. They would ride away on two horses, procured from Louisa knew not where. Or: She would set explosives next to the wall of the prison and when they blew open a hole in the outer wall, Will would escape and she would lead him back to Texas and Fredericksburg! Her thoughts made it all seem so easy.

How foolish you are, Louisa! she thought. Getting Will out of that Yankee prison will not be as easy as you think. And getting him all the way back to Texas will be even harder!

She tried to quell these negative thoughts, but they had a way of creeping into her mind at the worst possible times.

Finally, they were there! Corinth, Mississippi! Now all she had to do was find Will and formulate a plan.

First, she must accompany Major Blackmon, the doctor in charge of their group, when he reported in to Colonel Ainsworth, the commanding officer in charge of the base hospital.

That accomplished, Colonel Ainsworth ordered them to their quarters. Their duties would begin at dawn the next day. Louisa stood watching Colonel Ainsworth; she hadn't picked a nickname for him yet, but was getting close. She was considering "Teeth" because he had huge yellow horse teeth in his large red horseface.

His dark blue uniform was rusty with age, rumpled and worn; his crushed officer's cap sat askew on his head. Louisa glanced at his hands — large, as expected, and exceedingly dirty. Would he wash them, before operating on the next torn and bloody soldier? Louisa doubted it.

As though he had sensed her scrutiny, Doctor Ainsworth pointed a finger at her.

"You, orderly, stow your gear in the barracks and then get yourself over to the hospital and report to Doctor Blackmon. You others, do the same." He turned away, expecting no answer, only to be obeyed.

Louisa gave a half-hearted salute to his back and said, "Yes, sir, right away, sir!"

Billy giggled. "Louis, yer tongue's goin' to get ya in big trouble one of these days!"

The orderlies silently followed Louisa and Billy to the barracks and stood looking around at their new quarters.

The "barracks" was a line of crudely constructed buildings, built by the Yankee soldiers out of lumber stripped from deserted buildings in Corinth. There were holes in the roof and missing boards on the sides so that the weather, rain or cold wind or heat, was always with them as they tried to sleep. Narrow cots lined the walls and as Louisa sat on one and bounced, she realized the "mattresses" were stuffed with corn cobs! Ugh! Her back hurt, just thinking about it. She picked her cot by checking the ceiling for holes above her head.

An odor of rancid grease hung heavy in the air. Louisa realized that the mess tent was just behind the barracks. We'll have to put up with all those awful smells, night and day, she thought, wrinkling her nose.

She put her bedroll under her cot and straightened her rumpled uniform coat. She had to wear it always, even in this humid heat; her last three gold coins were still sewn in the lining and she daren't take a chance of someone discovering them.

"C'mon, Louis," Billy hollered, waiting at the barracks entrance. "Everybody's gone but us, while ya been lollygaggin' and dreamin'! Never seen such a feller for lollygaggin' and dreamin'!"

"I'm coming, Billy," Louisa said, setting her cap straight on her head, after scratching at the lice in her hair. Wouldn't Tina die, she thought, if she knew how I am living? But, even with the lice and chiggers and filth and disease all around me, I have never felt so alive! To be able to help someone who needs you, to have some part in all this . . . this history. . . .

"Louis!"

"I'm coming, Billy," she answered, hurrying to catch up with the others who had already entered the Tishomingo Hotel which had been converted into a hospital.

Louisa gasped as she took in the sights and sounds — and the smells — of the two-story brick hospital. The huge former ballroom of the hotel held narrow cots lined up in rows, each with a soldier, sick or wounded, lying in it, looking to the newcomers to help them.

Their calls and cries were almost unbearable. How could anyone hope to ease the misery and suffering in this vast room? With the others Louisa walked through the ward, nodding and speaking to each soldier. With one difference: Louisa's eyes searched for one special face. Was Will in this room, suffering from typhoid as so many were, or some other, equally deadly ailment? Row after row passed by as she walked, but no Will did she see. Where was he?

By the end of the day she had walked through the entire place, looking, looking for her brother. He was not in this hospital. As she lay down on her corn cob mattress, her one sleazy blanket folded under her to soften it a bit, she had to admit defeat. If Will wasn't in the hospital, where could he have gone? Tired and lonely, she let her discouragement take over, and spent the night soaking the thin blanket with her tears.

Louisa's work with the typhoid patients kept her so busy during the day and so tired at night, she barely had time to mourn for the failure of her plan to find Will. How she would ever locate him, she could not guess. But for now, all these poor men needed much care.

First, she and Billy and the others in their group had to learn the symptoms of the dread typhoid fever.

"At the onset of the disease," lectured Colonel Ainsworth, "the patient's face becomes flushed, his eyes glassy and his tongue white or brownish color, with red-tipped edges. He experiences chills and an extremely high fever, often up to 105 degrees."

Louisa gasped. How awful. Could Will have contracted this horrible disease . . . and . . . died?

". . . and during the second week," the doctor continued, "a rash appears, usually on the abdomen, chest or back. The abdomen swells and is sore. By the third or fourth week, if the victim survives that long, the rash and other symptoms slowly disappear and the patient recovers."

Louisa sighed with relief. Some victims did recover then. Perhaps Will had been sent to another place after he improved? A million questions swirled around in her brain as she listened to the doctor tell of the care the patients must have. Since there was no cure for the disease, it must simply run its course. The only help the orderlies could give was sympathy, water to drink and the usual duties they performed everywhere: bathing, listening to delirious soldiers' rantings, and praying over the dead as they wheeled them to the dead-house.

There wasn't much that they could do.

Several weeks passed as Billy, Louisa and the others worked long hours, seven days a week, trying to help the sick. There seemed to be no let up in cases; sometimes Louisa felt like she would be in this building, caring for these boys, for the rest of her life. She rarely had a minute to herself, to rest or write home or go out to see the town. She heard the trains pulling in to the station next door to the hospital and listened to their whistles as they departed again for Memphis. How she longed to be on one of those trains, headed for home. She was so tired.

"Louis, m'friend," Billy said one day, "feel me head. Do ya think I have a fever, eh? I don't feel so tip-top."

Louisa gasped as she felt Billy's forehead. He was burning with fever. When she made him stick out his tongue, there were the tell-tale signs. Billy had tyhoid!

Doctor Ainsworth ordered him to bed and assigned Louisa to his care, a job she would have done without orders. Suddenly she realized how much she had come to depend on the funny little man for companionship.

She pulled her cot up beside his, so that she could hear him if he needed her during the night. As he worsened, his fever sky-high and his mind roving, she prayed that he might be spared.

Her prayers were in vain. Billy Yost, private in the United States Army, Orderly Corps, died as Louisa watched over him, two weeks after he first became ill. Louisa felt as though she had lost yet another brother.

How could this sadness keep on, year after year, happening over and over again in so many families and to so many friends? Could anything justify all this suffering? Even the "rightness" of a cause? Both the North and the South were equally convinced of the "rightness" of their side. But both sides were losing all their bright, young men to the final victor in this bloody war: death!

Louisa decided to go home. She couldn't take it anymore. She had lost her chance to find Will, and now Billy was gone too. She would do what so many were doing these days. She would desert.

She wrote a letter to Tina, telling her about her failure to find Will and that she would be home soon. As she walked to the post office to mail the letter, her eyes widened with disbelief. Walking towards her, in tattered but recognizable rebel uniform, was a thin, emaciated soldier. He carried a haversack and seemed to be heading for the train station.

"Just a minute, soldier," Louisa called as she approached him. "Aren't you a little far from home? What are you doing in this Yankee stronghold?"

The soldier cringed and then clutched his haversack to his chest. "I have papers, soldier," he said. "I'm paroled and goin' home. I've had enough of y'all Yankees!"

"And where might home be?" Louisa asked, her heart lurching with homesickness as she thought she caught a slight German accent under the soldier's southern drawl.

"Texas, that's where," he said, his chin coming up in defiance, "and I can't wait to get there."

Louisa's voice came out in a whisper.

"Where in Texas, soldier?"

"You wouldn't have heard of it. It's just a small place, called Comfort. Comfort, Texas. That's my home."

"But I'm from Fredericksburg!" Louisa almost shouted. She wanted to hug the boy, but didn't dare. Someone might see them. It wouldn't be seemly!

"But why are you here? Where have you been?" Louisa had a thousand questions.

"I been up there a ways, in the federal prison, y'know, on the far side of town. Ja, there's a bunch of us up there. I'm mighty proud to be goin' home!"

"Prison? Did you say 'prison'?" Louisa wanted to hug the rebel soldier. Maybe that was where she'd find Will! She had been so sure he was in the hospital, she'd forgotten about the prison.

121

"Tell me, soldier, did you meet a German fellow named Will von Scholl in that prison?" Louisa held her breath.

"Will? Ja, he's been my buddy all this time. I hated to leave him there, but he wasn't chosen for the parole, that's all. Why, fella, d'y'all know each other?"

"Yes," whispered Louisa, her throat so constricted she could hardly speak. "Tell me, is he all right?"

"Oh, ja, he is all right. The Yankees don't like to parole the well ones who could go right back and fight some more. Me, I got me this minié bullet in my leg, but I wouldn't let 'em amputate, so now I'll be gimpy all my life, but at least I have two legs to stand on! Anyway, I'm no good for the army, so the Yanks let me go home.

"Nice talkin' to you, soldier," the rebel boy said when Louisa didn't speak. He started on down the street, limping, and gave her a half-wave. "I prob'ly won't see you again. I leave here tomorrow on the noon train. I can't wait to see Texas again!"

Louisa nodded, her head in a whirl. She had to find the prison and search for Will. She turned to see the Texas boy walking away from her.

"Wait!" she called. "Tell me where the prison is. I must go there and find your friend Will. And, please, tell me your name."

He turned back and smiled for the first time. "My name's Fritz Bauer . . . from Comfort, Texas. And the prison is over that-a-way," he said, pointing. "You can't miss it. It's a huge blockade. Must be a thousand or more prisoners there, I reckon."

"Thank you, Fritz," Louisa said, a lump in her throat at the thought of his name, the same as Fred's had been when the family still lived in Germany. When they came to Texas, before Louisa was born, Tina had renamed him Fred . . . and Wilhelm had become Will! But thinking of Fred still hurt. "Thank you again . . . danke," she repeated, "and good luck. . . ."

She watched Fritz Bauer until he rounded the corner and was out of sight. Now she must face a frightening fact. Her last chance to find Will, and to rescue him, was upon her. Was there any possibility at all that she could do it? Had she been fooling herself into thinking she could accomplish something that might be impossible?

She felt a chill, even as she perspired in the heat of the late afternoon.

Chapter Fourteen

The next morning Louisa found it easy to slip away from the hospital. Often the doctors left the hospital to the orderlies and went off to the Corinth Hotel to play cards and dine with ladies of the town. She walked in the general direction the young secesh soldier had pointed and, after about fifteen minutes of winding around the dirt streets, she found herself at the prison.

The prison! It was huge, much larger than Louisa had imagined. A high wooden fence surrounded it; a little more than half-way up the fence was a wooden walkway, about three feet in width. For the sentries to walk their rounds, Louisa decided.

How can I possibly get into this place, she wondered. And, worse, how can I ever get Will out? Or even find him? This would take some serious thinking.

She took one long, last look at the place that held her brother prisoner and turned back toward town and the hospital. I'll be back, Will, she promised.

As she walked to the center of Corinth, with its wooden buildings and dusty, dirt streets, she noticed some Union soldiers guarding cotton bales across from the Corinth Hotel. Some local farmers had evidently sold their cotton to the Yankees! She felt sorry for them if Confederate renegades, such as Duff, found out who they were!

As she thought of Duff — and home — she stopped dead still in the middle of the street. How stupid I am, she thought! How could I have not thought of it . . . what time did he say . . . noon? . . . Oh, I hope I'm in time. . . .

She was running now, toward the train station next to the hospital. She prayed the officers wouldn't see her. She had to get to the station before the train pulled out. The big engine, facing West, was idly puffing small spurts of smoke from its stack, warmed up and ready to go.

Louisa ignored the painful stitch in her side and raced past the engine and the coal car and grabbed the hand rail of the first passenger car she reached. Jumping up onto the platform, she pulled the heavy door open and entered the car. Frantically, she looked on both sides of the aisle as she raced through the car, onto the next platform and into the second car.

There he was: the boy from Comfort, Texas . . . what was his name? Fritz, she remembered at once, but the last name wouldn't come.

"Fritz," she panted, breathless from her chase. "Fritz, thank goodness you haven't left yet!"

"Why, howdy, private," the soldier named Fritz said, with a grin. "You're the fella wanted to know about Will, aren't you?"

"Yes," Louisa said, searching for words that would make sense to this young man. "I wonder if you'd do me a big favor?"

"Why, whatever I can do for a fellow Texan, I'll sure be glad to do." Fritz grinned and motioned for Louisa to sit beside him.

"No, there isn't time. The train is almost ready to leave. Please, find Will's family . . . they live south of Fredericksburg on the Bear Creek. Tell them he is well and hopes to see them soon. Tell them . . . that . . ." Louisa tried to gather her thoughts together, "they must go to Jefferson on Big Cypress Creek and wait there. No matter

126

how long, they must wait for Will. He will come, I promise. Will you tell them that?" Louisa paused, out of breath.

"Ja, sure, I will tell them. But I told you the Yankees won't give Will a parole. How can he get out of the prison?"

"Never mind. Just give them that message. And tell them that you talked to me, Louis Robinson. They'll remember me."

"All aboard!" the engineer shouted once, then again. "All aboard!"

"Goodbye, Fritz," Louisa called as she clambered down the train steps, "and thank you . . . danke schoen!"

She stood on the side of the street watching the train pull out. How close she had come to missing the opportunity to send word about Will to Tina and Papa and the children! She could imagine their faces when Fritz whatever-his-name-was gave them her message.

Grinning widely as she pictured the scene, she entered the hospital. Its sights and sounds and smells almost overpowered her after the morning's fresh air and happy moments with Fritz. Would she ever get to leave all this behind? She was so tired of the misery, of the frustration and grief.

Louisa spent a sleepless night, trying to think of a way to rescue Will as she listened to the rain on the roof, hearing the splattering drops of water hit the floor, or some poor soldier's face, as it found every loose or missing shingle on the roof. She was grateful that she had thought to check the condition of the ceiling before choosing her bunk.

I hope I can use as good judgment when I decide how to get into — and out of — that prison, she thought as she drifted into a troubled sleep sometime near dawn.

With the blue sky beaming through the holes in the roof, Louisa awoke, her plan in place. Papa had been right when he used to tell her to "sleep on it and it will come to you" when she went to him with a problem. It had "come" to her, during the damp dark hours, without her even knowing when it happened!

First, she must locate Will. As she hurried about her morning duties, she wondered how best to go about it. The key to her success lay tucked into the lining of her coat: the three gold coins! Guards could be bribed. Disguises could be bought. Train tickets were there for the exchange of a few dollars.

It was only a matter of days until Louisa, with her first gold coin exchanged for dollars at the Corinth bank, had found a guard who liked to gamble and who would take her to Will! How easy it is all turning out to be, she thought, amazed. Her heart soared as they walked past dozens of prisoners, in all stages of despair, until they reached the last row of bunks in the long hall.

There he was! Will! After all these long months she had really found him. Louisa stood for a moment, trying to slow her racing heart, to catch her breath, drinking in the sight of her brother. He sat, thin and drawn looking, his shoulders bent, reading from a ragged-looking newspaper.

As soon as the guard, holding fast the coins Louisa had given him, left on his way no doubt to the nearest poker game, Louisa cleared her throat. Hesitantly she spoke.

"Is there any news of Fredericksburg, Texas, in that paper, soldier?"

Will's head jerked up. For a moment he stared at her, his face gone white. Then, coming to his feet, he whispered, "Fred?"

Louisa laughed. "Oh, Will, don't you recognize me? It's Louisa, not Fred!"

"No . . . it can't be . . . Louisa's a sweet young girl . . . you're a soldier, a man! Why are you trying to fool me . . . you look like Fred . . . who are you anyway?"

Will brushed his forehead with his tattered sleeve. He shook his head. Louisa put her hand on his shoulder.

"Will, look carefully at me. Beneath all the dirt and grime and the cut hair and the Yankee uniform is your baby sister, Louisa. It's true, I promise you! And I have come to find you and take you home. Speak softly . . . no one must suspect I'm anything more than I look: a Yankee orderly, here to help the ailing prisoners. My 'name' is Louis Robinson."

"Oh, Lord, it's true, isn't it? You really are my little sister, aren't you?" Will shook his head in disbelief. "How did you manage to find me? How long have you been in that miserable looking uniform, a Yankee one at that?"

Louisa smiled. She was aching to take Will into her arms, to hug and comfort him, but she didn't dare take the chance. She couldn't risk discovery at this stage of her plans. Instead, she stood back and looked at her brother. He was so thin, so gaunt. His fair hair hung in bedraggled clumps, greasy and dark from lack of soap and water. His clothes were mere tattered remnants of the brave southern uniform he had once been so proud to wear. But the biggest and saddest change was in his eyes. Their intense blue seemed to have faded; they held knowledge that no man should be burdened with — sadness and defeat clouded what once had been clear and sure.

"Oh, Will," Louisa whispered. "What have you gone through? What has this awful war done to you?"

Will shook his head. Tears streamed down his cheeks now, as he realized fully what had happened. His sister was here with words of hope . . . hope that he might leave this place and go *home!* Was it possible? Or was it a dream? Louisa could read the thoughts in his mind as if they were in her own. "Yes, my dear brother, we are going home! I promise you.

"Have hope. You will see Tina and Papa soon . . . oh, yes, and Melissa too!" Funny how she always forgot Will's wife!

"About Melissa, Louisa . . . Louis," Will said with sadness in his voice, "She wrote me a letter when I was taken prisoner and said that she couldn't wait any longer. She needed a husband at home with her, to take care of her. She was terrified that the Yankees would come to Texas and she would be in great danger of her life. She wants a divorce so that she can marry some big cotton plantation owner, an old man who didn't take himself off to war!"

Louisa sat, speechless. She had never admired Melissa and her shallow, conceited airs, but she had never expected her to do something so terrible to Will.

"Oh, Will," she said, "I'm so very, very sorry!"

"Never mind," Will said, resignation in his voice. "It may be for the best. Melissa was never truly happy with me. I wasn't ambitious enough for her." He sighed. "I shall miss her. . . ." He sat, thinking private thoughts that Louisa had no right to know. She waited for her brother to recover himself. He straightened up and looked at her again.

"And Fred?" he said, his voice firm again. "Where is Fred, Louisa? Did he join the Confederacy as I told him to? Or is he in the Union blue like you have on?" A bitter note crept into Will's voice.

"Shh, Will, remember I am Louis Emil Robinson, an orderly at the Corinth Army Hospital. There is so much to tell you, and so little time. I'll come back soon. I promise. Now I must go . . . those prisoners over there are looking at us with much curiosity."

"I hate to see you go . . . Louis . . . hurry back, will you, please?" The pleading in Will's voice broke Louisa's heart. Where was the old Will, so sure of himself and of his beliefs? What had happened to have broken his spirit so?

She knew she had to leave . . . she couldn't trust herself to tell Will about Fred just yet. She would break down and sob on his shoulder, a luxury she couldn't afford right now.

"I'll be back as soon as I can arrange everything, Will, I promise." With those words she turned and walked back the way she had come, trying to ignore the calls of the other prisoners to talk to them, to take messages to their loved ones, to bring them food or water. She thought she would never reach the doorway of the long hall and escape their pitiful pleas.

All Louisa could think of for the next several days was Will. She made plans and then rejected them so fast she couldn't even remember which were the best of the lot. She wished Billy Yost were still alive. He had been a loyal friend and she might have shared her secret with him. He might have known what to do.

She had many regrets about Billy. The worst was that she had learned so little about him. She didn't even know where he was from, or what family he left behind. I was too wrapped up in my own troubles to bother with anyone else, Louisa thought with shame. I hope I never do that to anyone again. I hope I can be more helpful and understanding to others and less concerned with myself and my own problems.

As though to test her resolution, she met and immediately liked the new orderly, sent in from New Orleans on the hospital ship which brought more patients for Louisa and the others to tend.

The new man's name was George. He was tall, soft-spoken and handsome . . . and he was black. Louisa had never known a black person before. The few who lived in Fredericksburg were free blacks who stayed off to themselves, probably to avoid confrontations with the likes of Duff and his raiders. She had seen many black people, of course, in New Orleans and coming up the Mississippi, but always from afar. She had never before had a chance to meet one and get acquainted. She welcomed the opportunity. I want to know how different and how alike we are, she thought. She introduced herself to George.

George had no last name. He refused to take the name of his former master as so many freedmen did.

"He was no good," George said, a small frown flitting across his features. "Why would I wanna go name myself after a no-good white man? Onliest reason I's free is 'cause he died an' his widow, a good woman, gave me an' my family our freedom!"

"But didn't the proclamation Lincoln wrote in January make you a free man, George?" Louisa had never figured out that puzzle.

"No, sir, it shore didn't. None of the darkies up h'yere in the North is free yet. Neither is my brothers in the South. Not till Gen'ral Lee surrenders and they change the constitution! But I was already a freedman, almost two years now. I got the papers to prove it, should they's ask me!"

Some of the orderlies and a few of the doctors treated George as though he were invisible. They neither spoke to him nor included him at the mess table. It was as though he didn't exist.

Louisa could not stand this injustice. She took it upon herself to praise George, to talk to him about the hospital, the patients and the war. If it made the others uncomfortable, good! She continued her efforts on George's behalf.

Then, she discovered, to her surprise, George had become a real friend. She really cared what happened to him and hoped he felt the same about her. She enjoyed their long discussions about the world and its problems; she looked forward to the times George worked the same shift and they could share a laugh at some patient's expense or a tear when they lost another one. She felt a little sense of pride at having a black man for a friend.

Then a sickening thought occurred to her. I am as bad as those bigots out there, she thought. Why should I be "proud" of my "generosity" at making this man my friend? He, after all, was equally generous to me, accepting my friendship and offering his. He is a good man and that is all I need to know.

Louisa yearned to confide in someone, someone she could trust, about her plans for Will. She sought George out one afternoon when no one else was in the barracks. He was lying on his cot, reading the Corinth army newspaper, *The Chanticleer*.

"Paper says war shouldn't last too much longer, Louis," George said as Louisa walked up to his bunk. "Maybe we gets to go home pretty soon, huh?"

"I hope so, George," Louisa answered. "Uh, George, forgive me, but . . . I don't know how to ask this . . . uh, where did you learn to read?"

"Ah, my white young friend," George answered, grinning. "I c'n write too. What you think of that, huh?"

"Well, that's wonderful, George, but how . . . where?"

"Used to sneak behind the white chil'rens schoolhouse on the plantation. Thin walls made it easy to hear, and I found books the white young'uns lost in the woods. Soon as you know it, I could read them books, and then I found a writin' book and learned that too. Pretty good fer an ol' black boy, huh?"

"Very good, George," Louisa said, grinning. "You probably would have gotten the highest grade in the class."

Louisa made a decision. She needed help with Will and who better than George to trust?

Carefully, Louisa explained about Will, her plan for him to escape and how she needed George's help. He looked at her for a long time and then nodded.

"I'm proud you tol' me all this, Louis, or whatever yo' name might be. I reckon you must have a right nice female name, bein's how you're a right nice female, ain't it so?"

133

Aghast, Louisa stopped in her tracks. How could he have known? Was it so obvious? Would anyone else guess?

"George!" she barely got the word out of her constricted throat. "However did you know?"

"I didn't know fer sure, lady, but I jes watched the way you worked with those hurt and sick boys in there — and I knew, tha's all! But don' worry your head about it . . . old George will never tell nobody. Nossir, he won't."

"Thanks, George, but I really do need your help now," Louisa said, studying the dark face for signs. "I've got to get my brother out of that prison and back to Texas. Will you help me? I know it'll mean terrible trouble for you if we're caught!"

"Trouble ain't never been a stranger to me, Louis — I'm gonna keep callin' you that, so's not to slip up in front of someone! 'Course I'll help you, jes you tell me what you need done . . . and it's done."

"Oh, thank you, George," Louisa said, "I knew you were someone I could trust.

"Here's my plan. . . ."

"Sounds like a mighty fine plan to me, Louis," George said when Louisa finished, breathless. "Jes you tell me what you need, like I said."

That night Louisa slept deeply. Her last thought was about her plan to free Will. It was in place and all thought out. And George believed it would work, too, she thought happily. By tomorrow night Will would be free and they would be on their way to Texas.

But the next morning, all her plans had to change.

Chapter Fifteen

Louisa awoke slowly, aware that something was wrong. She felt disconnected, strange; her throat was on fire; her head spun. She groped to the wall where the water pitcher sat and gulped several swallows from the communal cup.

I can't get sick, not now, she thought, dismayed. Today I'm going to get Will out of prison and away from here. She staggered back to bed and lay panting from the exertion. If she could only sleep for several hours. . . .

No! She pulled herself upright, forced on her boots, then tried to stand. She nearly fainted. She had to keep going . . . didn't dare get sick . . . doctor mustn't examine her . . . all would be lost if she was found out now. . . .

As she collapsed to the floor she felt strong hands lifting her and placing her on her cot. George! Thank goodness . . . he would take care of her . . . he wouldn't let the doctors . . .

She struggled to sit up. "George, don't leave me," she pleaded. "You mustn't let them examine me. Promise me!"

"Yes, Louis, I understan'," George said. "I'll surely take good care of you and you'll be up and about in no time a'tall. Meantime, doctors don't need to know nothin' about this. You knows they never sets foot inside these h'ere barracks.

"Now, let me see that tongue."

He's as bossy as Tina, Louisa thought, feeling very

weak as she stuck out her tongue. George said, "Mmmmm," and felt her forehead.

"Well, what is it? Why are you saying, 'Mmmm' like that?" Louisa demanded.

"It's the typhoid, Louis, you might jes' as well up an' face it. Your tongue be as white as your face and all furry lookin', with a bright red border! And you're burnin' up with fever. You not be goin' to Texas today or for many days, I reckon." George shook his head with sorrow.

"Oh, no!" Louisa wailed. "What about my plans for Will? What shall we do? Think of something, George!"

"Bes' thing, jest wait it out," George said, his head cocked to one side. "I'll see if'n I kin sneak in to see your brother, tell him what happen. He'll unnerstan'."

Louisa closed her eyes to stop the tears from flowing. She had no choice but to do what George suggested. But, she thought in despair, it takes several weeks to recover from typhoid — if you recover! How can we wait that long? Tina and the others will be sitting there in Jefferson, wondering where we are. And poor Will. He'll be so disappointed.

Louisa had no choice but to lie back and let time decide her fate. More people died from typhoid than survived it, and she wondered if she had come so close to rescuing Will . . . and perhaps to die alone in this dingy barracks. Alone, except for George.

Her days and nights ran together, the fever taking her into delirium. Occasionally she was aware of George forcing some weak soup down her throat, or carrying her to the latrine where he stood guard so she could be alone. As from a great distance, she heard him tell grumbling soldiers, "That fella in there has the typhoid. Now y'all wouldn't wanna get close to him, would you? Jes let him be. Only take a minute. Then I takes him back to bed. But first one tells the doctors we got a case of typhoid in this h'yere barracks has to answer to George, you hear?"

136

The secret was kept; no doctor came near the barracks and George managed to handle both his and Louisa's duties without anyone missing her.

Finally, she knew that she was going to live. She felt the fever receding, the weakness lessening and an overall paralysis of the spirit fading. She had known she could do it! Except, she couldn't have, not without George's help. No brother could have done more.

"How can I ever thank you, George," Louisa said one morning as she tried to get the week-long tangles out of her hair. "You saved my life. And saved my plan for Will too. As soon as I get stronger, I'll get us out of here and get to Jefferson and the family. But, I'll never, never forget what you've done for me."

George ducked his head, but not before Louisa caught a suspicious glistening in his eyes.

"You were friend to me first, Louis, and I never forget that, either! Y'know, you talked some in your fever . . . about your family and all . . . I know about Fred and how he die because he don't believe in slavery. You come from good stock, Louis." Pausing, with some embarrassment George went on, "If'n you really wants to do somethin' for me, I know somethin' I'd be most proud to have. . . ." His voice trailed off in embarrassment.

"Tell me, George! If it's possible, I'll surely get it for you!" Louisa said with excitement.

"You already have it, my friend," George said. "It's your name. I'd deem it most proud if'n I could take Robinson for my last name."

"Oh, George, I'd 'deem it most proud' if you'd take the name of Robinson! All my family will be most honored to have you share our name. Thank you, George, for the wonderful compliment! A person's last name is very, very important. I hope you wear ours with much happiness!"

"George Robinson! It do sound good, don' it?" George, a huge smile wreathing his face, left Louisa to make his rounds of the hospital.

When he returned a few hours later, the smile was gone. A deep frown of worry had replaced it. Louisa knew something had happened. A small prickle of dread slithered down her spine. With great effort she sat up, to face whatever George had to say. Her head spun, and she had to fight the urge to ease back into bed.

"What is it, George? Something's happened. Tell me, please."

"Bad news, Louis," George said, always careful to keep up the pretense that Louisa was who she pretended to be. "I heard the doctors talkin' in the ward."

"Well, what is it, George?" Louisa asked, trying to find the strength to stand up.

"They're fixin' to send us off . . . all the orderlies bein' sent to fightin' places, where we can he'p the wounded, 'stead of worryin' over these h'yere sick ones."

"But, the typhoid epidemic . . . and the other illnesses these boys suffer from . . . who'll tend to them, George?" Louisa thought of all the men in the hospital, sick, some dying, needing her help and that of the other orderlies.

"Well, that's jest it, Louis," George said, his head shaking as though he himself couldn't believe what he had to say. "They's sendin' in nurses, *women* nurses! Some female named Dorothea Dix is bringin' in a whole troop of them female nurses to take our place! You ever heared of sech a thing?"

"But I've heard of Dorothea Dix, George! She is an angel of mercy. She goes all over the country showing the doctors how good the women are at nursing, and she trains girls to be nurses, and she fought the conditions of the insane asylums and she. . . ."

"Whoa, there, Louis," George interrupted. "What you don't unnerstan' about this 'angel of mercy' is that she's a-comin' tomorrow! And we have to be out of h'yere by day affer tomorrow! And you not up and about yet."

Louisa went pale. What about Will? How would she get him out, if she herself was to be sent away?

"We'll just have to do it by tomorrow, then, George," she said, purpose in her voice.

"Ayyy, jes' listen to Private Robinson talk, lak he kin jes' git up and go these days!" George laughed and shook his head.

"Well, I'm going to, whether you help me or not. So . . . how about it? Are we in this together or what?" As she threw the challenge at George, Louisa pulled herself up and drew a deep breath.

Dizzy, she clutched George's arm.

"Well?" she repeated.

"I'll he'p you, Private Robinson," George said, grinning.

"Good for you, Private Robinson," Louisa answered, slapping George on the back. Surprised, he half-fell forward, then sat on the bunk, his grin even wider.

"Only have one li'l problem," he said, watching Louisa's face. "You's in no condition to go runnin' around rescuin' no brother! I'll do the plan and you'll wait here for me. Then we'll steal away like two horse thieves, all right?"

"No, no, no!" Louisa nearly shrieked, causing the nearest soldier to look her way. Everyone avoided her since George had mentioned she had typhoid. She lowered her voice. "This is my job and I intend to see it finished. You can help, that's all, do you understand?"

George nodded, laughing silently. His patient had certainly taken a sudden turn for the better.

The next morning Louisa was up at dawn. She felt weak and a little nauseated, but she gamely joined the other orderlies and doctors in the main dining hall to "meet Miss Dix." So the order sent around the night before had read.

There she was, the woman Louisa had admired for a long time, since reading about her in the newspapers. She had been all over the world and had made many very big men very angry, but had gotten results, nevertheless. Many insane asylums were no longer inhumane and a disgrace to their countries. Now she was taking on army doctors and hospitals, Louisa thought with amusement, and I just wager I know who'll come out the winner!

"Men!" Colonel Ainsworth, "Teeth," bellowed in his most officious voice. "This morning you have a real honor in store for you. I would like you to meet Miss Dorothea Dix, Superintendent of Women Nurses. She will be bringing her female nurses to this hospital in order to free you male orderlies for battle areas. Please give her your utmost respect and cooperation." "Teeth" didn't look happy about this new order of things. Louisa was sure he was far from convinced that the female nurses were a good thing . . . for the army or for army doctors!

All eyes turned to look at the woman standing a little apart from Colonel Ainsworth. She appeared to be around sixty years old, Louisa thought, her hair combed flat and drawn severly into a knot at the back of her head, and she blushed when "Teeth" introduced her! According to what Louisa had read of Dorothea Dix, she made doctors and other officers tremble and back down before her. Yet she blushed!

She murmured a greeting to the orderlies and turned to leave the room. Just then a young sergeant called out, "Miss Dix, would you answer me a question, please, ma'am?"

Miss Dix turned and blushed again. She nodded her head.

"Well, Miss Dix, ma'am," the soldier said, "I got a sister back home in Ohio what wants in the worst way to be a nurse. Do you think she could come and be one of your nurses, ma'am? What would she have to do?"

"Well, young man," Dorothea Dix spoke firmly, despite her flushed face and shy manner, "I will quote from my directive on nursing and you can judge whether your sister would qualify to be one of my staff.

"I quote: 'No woman under thirty years need apply to serve in government hospitals. All nurses are required to be very plain-looking women. Their dresses must be brown or black, with no bows, no curls, no jewelry, and no hoop-skirts.' Does that answer your question, soldier?"

"Yes, ma'am, it sure does. My sister is eighteen and, even with a black dress and no curls or hoops, there ain't no way she'd be called 'plain looking'!"

Laughter filled the room. "Teeth" shouted for attention and the soldiers quieted down, but not before Miss Dix had blushed furiously once again.

Louisa and George filed out of the mess hall with the rest of the men.

"Come on, George, step lively," Louisa said. "We've got a lot to do before tomorrow morning when those 'plain-looking' ladies make their appearance and displace us."

Chuckling, George followed Louisa out of the main building and over to their barracks. They did indeed have a lot to do by tomorrow morning!

Chapter Sixteen

Just before dawn Louisa shook George awake.

"George! Wake up," she whispered. "We've got to work fast. Sit up, sit up, so that I know you're awake and hearing me!"

" Wha . . . Oh, Louis, why you wakin' me up when it still night?" George rubbed his eyes with his big hands and reluctantly sat up. "What is it? Trouble?"

"No, George," Louisa said, an excited edge to her voice, "no trouble. Today we rescue Will! Do you know how long I've been waiting for this day?

"Here's what I want you to do. You are going to help me, aren't you, George?"

"Oh, yes, I sure am goin' help you," George said, wide awake now and grinning. "You say it, I does it!"

"Good. Here's a gold coin, worth a lot of money — I'm not sure how much. But it's enough to buy two horses and a wagon and some supplies for a 'journey out west'! And here's a letter, authorizing you to make the purchases, in case someone gives you trouble.

"We'll need blankets and food and feed for the horses, everything to get us to Jefferson. Also, please get me a calico dress, shawl and sunbonnet. And some talcum powder. All right, George?"

"You mean, you trusting George with all that gold money?" Disbelief showed in George's eyes. "Nobody's never trusted George like that, never!"

143

"Of course I'm trusting you! Aren't you my friend? Didn't you save my life? What a silly thing to think about now when we have so much to do, George!" Louisa pretended not to see the tears well up in George's eyes.

"Take the wagon and supplies to the livery stables where we can pick them up later. Here, take my bedroll with you, and leave it on the wagon. Now, scoot! There's lots to be done!"

"I'se scootin', I'se scootin'!" George said, laughing happily.

After George left, Louisa bustled about, making her morning rounds of the patients, eating her sparse breakfast, trying to act normal when her heart was racing and she felt a little faint. Could she pull it off?

At nine o'clock she stood at the back of the hospital, where she knew the dead wagon headed for the prison would have to stop for a moment before starting its gruesome journey. Every other morning the wagon set out empty for the prison and came back, often full, of corpses of those who had died since the last trip. The corpses were dumped in the dead-house at the hospital, to be buried in shallow, mass graves sometime that week.

Louisa was going to be aboard that wagon on its way to the prison.

Right on time, the wagon pulled up to the back door of the hospital. The driver jumped down, threw the reins over the porch rail and ran up the steps and into the building. Quickly Louisa crawled inside the wagon and curled up in a corner. The wagon, covered with canvas, was dark. The driver would never notice her.

After what seemed a long time but what was probably only a few minutes, Louisa heard the driver climb into the wagon and click his teeth at the horses, who obediently started up at a slow pace. The driver was in no hurry to complete his grim duty. Louisa wished he were; the stench of previous dead bodies almost overwhelmed her. But, she thought, I can stand anything if it means freeing Will from that prison!

As the driver pulled up at the prison wall, was admitted by the guard and let through the gate, Louisa held her breath. She only would have a short moment to escape the wagon, between the time the driver stopped the horses and when he'd throw back the canvas, ready to receive his sad cargo. She crouched, ready to jump.

The wagon stopped. Louisa pushed the tarp out of her way and glanced quickly around, making sure no one from the prison was around anywhere, leapt down from the wagon and flew to the protection of a small, empty guard house beside the door. When the driver pounded on the door and showed his papers to the sergeant who opened it cautiously, Louisa followed him through the door, pointing to the driver as if to say, "I'm with him." The driver, intent on getting the job done, didn't notice her behind him. When the prison guard was out of hearing, she cleared her throat loudly.

"Who're you?" the driver demanded. "Where'n dickens did you come from? Gave me a start, you did!"

"Sorry," Louisa said, grinning. "I'm stationed here at the prison. They told me to help you find the bodies and bring 'em out. I'll accompany them, and you, back to the hospital. Then I'm on furlough and will take the train home for a few days."

"Lucky fella!" The driver was a husky man, given to a tic in his left eye. "Wall, c'mon then. Let's get this over with."

"Why don't you go on ahead," Louisa suggested. "I just remembered somethin' I left in the barracks. I'll join you in a few minutes. You start at this end, don't you? And work your way back?"

"Yep, that's how I do it. Hurry up with your business. I don't like to stick around this place very long."

Louisa ran down the halls, trying to remember where in that huge prison Will was. Her eyes watched for guards; she had to speak with Will before anyone knew she was there.

Her luck held. She saw Will, sitting dejectedly on his cot, staring at his hands.

"Psst, Will," Louisa whispered. "I'm here and you've got to listen quickly. We only have a few moments."

Will looked up, unseeing at first, then a big grin spread across his thin face.

"Louisa!. . . . Louis . . . you're alive! Thank God! What's happening?"

Quickly Louisa told Will what to do and, understanding at last, he grasped her hand and nodded, unable to speak.

Without a word, he collapsed onto the prison's stone floor. He lay still. Louisa turned and ran out the way she had come.

"Driver! Come this way! There's another one for you. Just keeled over. Dead as a bug. May as well take him on this trip."

"I'm comin'! I'm comin'!" the driver answered, annoyed at having yet another body to transport. "Where you been, I thought you was goin' to he'p me !"

"Oh, I was s'posed to check the rounds and gather any new bodies up. Like this one here. Still warm, he is, but gone, that's fer sure! Give me a hand with him, will ya?"

The driver and Louisa carried Will's "body" out of the prison and into the wagon, now almost full of corpses in various degrees of decay. Louisa gagged. She pressed her nose into her sleeve. Poor Will. He had to lie there with the bodies crowded next to him and never make a move. Louisa was thankful that she would be riding outside the wagon with the driver.

How quickly Will had caught on to her plan! Now if things would go as well at the other end.

Back at the hospital the prison corpses were dumped onto the waiting shelves of the dead-house, joining the ones collected from the hospital. Louisa saw to it that Will's "body" was placed close to the outside doorway on the long slab. He never made a move and didn't even seem to be breathing. But, when Louisa put his hand on his chest he gave her fingers the slightest squeeze.

Now they had to wait for dark.

"Psst, Will," Louisa whispered as she entered the black interior of the dead-house. She had a handkerchief over her nose, but the stench still seeped through, gagging her. She heard a movement, then a low grown, and Will's low whisper, answering hers.

"Here, Sis, I can't get up. One of the bodies is wedged up against me and, if I move, the whole stack will roll down on top of me."

Ugh, Louisa thought, how gruesome! She took a deep breath, gritted her teeth and reached out in the darkness. She felt the cold body which kept Will trapped there in that hall of death. Pushing, she managed to move it away a few inches.

"All right, I'm free, Sis," Will whispered. "Give me a hand up; I'm pretty weak.

Groping in the still darkness of that dread place, Louisa found Will's hand, reaching for hers. With all the strength she could summon, Louisa pulled Will out of the mass of bodies and to a standing position. Silently, they hugged each other, Louisa too choked up to speak.

Will shuddered, as though trying to shake the smell and feel of death from his body and clothes. His hands, in Louisa's, felt almost as cold as those of the corpse she had just touched.

"Come on, Will, we have to get out of here. Can you walk?" Louisa wondered what she'd do if his answer was no.

147

"Yes, Sis," Will said, a small smile in his voice, "I could run, if it would get me away from this place!"

Haltingly they made their way to the door of the dead-house, Louisa thinking how glad she was never to have to enter it again. At the door they stopped, and she peered outside, in case someone was taking a late night walk. Seeing no one, she tugged on Will's arm, and they crept outside, both taking deep breaths of the nearly fresh air.

"Hurry, Will," she said, anxious now to finish her escape plan and be on their way. "We must get to the livery stable where George has left our wagon and horses.

"I really feel sad that I didn't get to say a proper good-bye to George. He has been a true friend and I'm going to miss him very much."

The livery stable was only a block from the hospital, but it was the longest block Louisa had ever traveled. She kept expecting a shout or gunfire or a demand that they stop and give an accounting of themselves . . . then all would be lost.

As they rounded the corner Louisa knew they were at the stable. She remembered where it was; she also smelled the familiar, pungent horse smell. It was like perfume after the nauseating odor of the dead-house.

She heard a sound! Stopping their progress by a pressure on Will's arm, she held her breath. Was it all to end here? So close to success? Motionless, she waited for another sound, some tell-tale movement, to show her the enemy.

"Louis?" a hoarse whisper from the darkness told her who the "enemy" was.

"George! What are you doing here? If you get caught you'll hang for treason." Louisa's relief was so great, she felt the need to scold — or she would start crying.

"Well, h'yere I be, so don' go talkin' of hangin'!" George sounded relieved, too, to know the strangers in the night were his friends, after all.

"Well, yes, you're here, and I'm really glad, George. Did you get everything? Here, help Will. He's pretty weak. Where's the wagon? Did you have enough money?"

"Whoa, there, Louis!" George said, laughing now as Louisa rattled on without stopping for breath. "Can't nohow answer all them questions at once!

"Com'on, get in this h'yere wagon and we talk as we go. Better to get some miles 'tween us and this place 'fore dawn!"

"Yes, you're right, George," Louisa answered. "Except for one thing: you are not going with us! You can't, much as I'd love it. If they caught you, you'd hang! We couldn't take such a chance."

"Wha . . . ? George not goin'?" The hurt and disappointment in his voice made Louisa want to cry. "How you gonna get 'long, without George? Huh?"

"It's not going to be easy, George, and I want you to know that you're the best friend I ever had. After this war is over, I want you to come to Texas. We'll be needing a partner in our Angora goat business. There's lots of money in mohair, plenty for all of us.

"But, for now," she went on, nearly in tears, "you've got to go back. I couldn't bear it if they caught you, a deserter! You know what they'd do to you! Please, George, don't make it harder for me than it already is!"

Silence lasted so long that Louisa began to think that George had slipped away into the night while she argued.

"I sees your point, Louis," he said, finally, sadness in his voice. "An' I'll stay. But only 'cause I sees that I might be a danger to you and Will h'yere. The Yankees wouldn't take kindly to nobody what helped a darky soldier escape!

"So I guesses it's goodbye for now, Louis. Remember ol' George Robinson, will you?"

Reaching out in the dark until she felt George's sleeve, Louisa took a step forward and threw her arms around him.

"Thank you for everything, George," she said, her voice trembling. "I meant what I said about coming to Texas after the war. Please. We need and want you there. Don't we, Will?"

Louisa held her breath, waiting for Will to speak. What would he say to this black man, her best friend, after owning men like him for so long?

"George," Will said, his voice unsteady, "how can I ever thank you for what you've done, both for my sister and for me? I would be honored to have you for a partner after this blasted war is over. You won't forget, will you?"

"I'd hardly forgets the two best folks I ever knew," George said. "An' y'all most likely will be seein' me, come this war is over and done with!

"Now, you better get along with you. It's startin' to lighten up over there in the east. God keep you safe, Louis."

"And you, George. I'll write you when we get home. Take good care of yourself." Tears were streaming down Louisa's face now. She gave George one last hug.

"My real name is Louisa Emily von Scholl, George. The Robinson belongs to my sister and her family. They will be most proud to know you carry their name too."

"Goodbye, then, Louisa Emily von Scholl," George said, pride in his voice. "You's the bravest one female I ever done met. And the best soldier! Take care. And, if I don' make it through this war, remember Private George Robinson, won' y'all?"

Louisa caught her breath as George backed away from her grasp and she heard his footsteps getting fainter and fainter. She prayed he'd be safe and that they'd meet again.

But now, the time she had waited for so long had come, and there was much to do before they could leave Corinth, Mississippi, far behind them.

"Come on, Will," she said, her heart full of mixed emotions, "let's get busy!

Chapter Seventeen

"Hurry, Will, skinny out of that ragged uniform and climb into these." Louisa pulled Fred's clothes out of her knapsack and shoved them in Will's direction. It was starting to get light now; they needed to rush.

As Will dressed, Louisa got out of her uniform, stiff with blood and sweat, smelly beyong belief and showing signs of extreme wear! The dead soldier who had worn this never dreamed that his uniform would be used for such a good cause!

She slid the brown cotton dress which George had bought over her head and sighed with relief to be a girl once again. Woman, she corrected herself. She could never call herself "girl" again — not after what she had seen and done these past several months.

She shrugged the shawl, a soft blue wool that smelled of cedar, around her shoulders and finger-combed her hair. The sunbonnet, obviously second-hand, was of a blue print cotton stuff. Like the dress, the material was inferior to calico, but would last until she got home.

Before rolling her uniform into a ball and hiding it inside a bale of the horses' hay, she tore the lining and retrieved her last gold coin. This she tied into a piece of the lining and sewed it into the hem of her skirt.

"Are you ready, Will?" Louisa asked her brother. The sun was beginning to show itself above the horizon, casting a pink glow over everything. What a wonderful way to start our homeward journey, Louisa thought, with the sun's bright rays to warm us and the blue sky above to give us cheer!

Will had been very quiet. Now that she could see him in the early light, she was stricken with sadness at how old and drawn he looked. Well, Tina would fatten him up at home — if there was any food to be had by now!

Louisa fished around in the bag of supplies until she found the can of talcum powder.

"Come over here, Will, I need to finish your disguise."

"Wha . . . What do you mean, disguise, Louisa? Aren't these clothes enough? I hope Fred could spare them for me."

Holding Will's head with one hand, Louisa sprinkled the talcum onto his hair. She rubbed it in and brushed the excess off his shoulders. The transformation was amazing! Will looked just like Papa! All he needed was a pipe!

"Now," Louisa said, with satisfaction, "you are my elderly father, ill and being taken to your son's home in Texas for care. Amazing what a change of clothes and gray hair can do!"

"Well, look at yourself," Will said, laughing. "What became of that brave, young orderly who did all the heroic things amidst death and danger? All I see" — his voice took on a bit of the old banter Will and Fred had used to tease her with so long ago — "is a fair, young lady who could stand a bath and hair-wash, but is quite handsome, nonetheless."

Louisa grinned and clucked to the horses, who knew her wishes immediately and started away from the empty livery stable at a slow walk. Another cluck, and they picked up the pace. Louisa felt a sudden need to get out of Corinth and away from possible capture.

They rode along in companionable silence for a half hour. When they were out in the countryside, Louisa felt a little safer. She let herself relax a bit; her neck was stiff from turning to see if they were being followed. So far, so good.

Now was as good a time as any, Louisa thought, to find out about the letter. Better to get it out in the open and talk about it.

She hesitated, then plunged ahead. "Will, did you get the letter I wrote you?" She held her breath.

"Did you write me a letter, Louisa?" Will asked. Then he went on, "I got a letter from a foolish girl who didn't quite understand the situation, but I forgave her for the things she said. I don't know anyone like that, anymore, only a very grown-up and heroic young woman who has saved my life!"

"Oh, Will, you do forgive me then? I'm so sorry I wrote those hateful words. I would have given anything if I hadn't!" Louisa reached over and squeezed her brother's hand.

"And I am sorry I was the cause of your unhappiness, Louisa. But now, we're together again, just like old times, ja?" Will said, laughing.

"I love you, Will," Louisa whispered, a great weight lifted from her shoulders.

Relaxed now, Louisa began telling him of the family, talking of friends and fun times they had had together in the good days before the war.

"Louisa," Will said, after a while, "you have told me about Papa and Tina and how big the twins are growing and how Emily likes coffee. You haven't mentioned Fred. I'm no longer angry at my younger brother, so why don't you want to talk about him?"

Louisa's heart sank. She hated to tell Will that Fred was dead, to break the spell of his happiness and relief at being free once again. But she knew she had to, sooner or later. She spoke slowly and haltingly, choosing her words with care.

153

"When we learned that you had joined the Confederate army, Will," she began, holding his hand in hers, "Fred was angry. All of us felt sad and worried, but Fred swore that he would never join the army to fight the southern slaveowners' war. I couldn't blame him; he had no interest in slavery or states' rights, like you did. He just wanted to raise his goats and lead a quiet life in our Texas hills.

"But, it was not that simple. The war caught up with us there in the Hill Country. Confederate renegades scoured the land for 'German traitors' and many of our friends and neighbors were hanged or their homes burned out."

"Oh, no, Louisa, how could that be? Jeff Davis would never have condoned such a thing!" Will's voice held shock and disbelief.

"Well, it was true. Jeff Davis was a long way from Texas. Duff and his men, and the others like him, didn't care what the president of the Confederacy, or General Lee, for that matter, might think. They went right on plundering and killing!"

"But, what does that have to do with Fred, Louisa? Surely he didn't approve of such activities?"

"No, of course not," Louisa spoke more sharply than she intended, "but it put Fred's life in danger every day. Those bands of renegades roamed the hills and finally, one day. . . ." Louisa caught her breath. How could she say it out loud? How could she tell Will what happened there on the hillside that awful day?

"One day? What, Louisa?" Will prodded.

"One of Duff's Raiders found us on the hillside, shearing a goat. He . . . he . . . killed Fred in cold blood, Will. Fred never had a chance!"

Will's face went deadly white. His hands clenched into fists and then smashed at the side rails of the wagon. His breath came in short gasps, and Louisa was afraid he was going to faint.

"Fred is dead?" Will whispered. Louisa nodded her head, tears streaming down her cheeks.

She dropped the reins, reached out her arms and he came into them, like a child who needed mothering, sobbing and moaning his loss.

They stayed that way for a long time, the horses making their patient way forward on the road to Jefferson. They had no care for the sadness of people; just let them rest sometimes and give them their hay at the end of the day. How lucky to be a horse, Louisa thought. You never see a horse cry!

Thinking silly thoughts about horses doesn't change anything, Louisa told herself, crossly. Fred is dead, and I will miss him forever. But we must make ourselves go on. Will must understand that.

With sympathy and understanding Louisa spoke in a soft voice to Will, trying to help him through his shock and sadness, trying to make him see that they must look to the future, not dwell on the past.

And, all the while, the horses patiently plodded on.

The next day was their big test. As they rode along the country road west of Corinth, Louisa spotted riders gaining on them, fast.

"Will, slump down, quick. Someone is coming. They might be soldiers from the prison! Remember you're my old papa, going home to Texas. Don't say anything; I'll talk to them. Your voice might sound too young."

Without looking back, Will took on the stance of an old man, slumping and snoozing in his seat. Louisa thought how easily he took her words and followed them without questioning her leadership. She felt quite proud of herself — until she saw the riders approaching. They were soldiers! Fear took over all other feelings, leaving her too weak to speak.

Then, that old, stubborn determination to get Will back home took over. She carefully reached behind her and got hold of the rifle, brought it onto the seat between her and Will and stealthily covered it with her blue shawl. She was glad it was her turn to drive. Will sat, silent, looking for all the world like the old man he was supposed to be.

"Howdy, ma'am," the first soldier, a sergeant, said, tipping his blue, slouch hat to Louisa.

"Hello, sergeant," Louisa said demurely, or what she thought sounded "demure"!

"Don't want to bother you none, ma'am, but we're hunting a couple soldiers from the barracks at Corinth. Would you have seen them, any chance? A young private, orderly at the hospital, who deserted, and a prisoner from the army prison."

"Why, no, we haven't," Louisa said in her most lady-like tone. "I'm taking my sick Papa to stay with my brother in Texas. I've been so truly worried about Papa, I really haven't noticed anyone on the road. I surely am sorry!"

Will sat, not moving. Louisa lowered her eyes, hiding her face with her sunbonnet and said a quick prayer that she had been convincing.

Her hand remained on the stock of the rifle beneath her shawl.

"Well, we're mighty sorry to have bothered you, ma'am, and I sure hope your pa makes the trip all right. He looks mighty weak to me.

"Best of luck to you. We'll be goin' along now."

He tipped his hat, his companion nodded and they spurred their horses and were off down the road.

Louisa sat very still, not believing it was all over. Then she heard Will heave a big sigh.

"You might just have to try out for a career as an actress in one of those stage plays, Louisa!" he said, laughing. "You were magnificent. Never heard you sound so innocent in my life!"

"Hush, Will! I was just doin' what I had to do, that's all!" Louisa said, blushing at the thought of becoming an actress! "Anyway, it worked, didn't it?"

"Yes, little sister, it worked . . . beautifully!" Will answered, pride in his voice. "You can put away the gun now."

"Oh, yes," Louisa said, a sheepish smile on her face.

The miles crept past, days followed days, and during the nights, sleeping under the starry skies, Louisa wondered what her future would hold. She thought about Helmut. She wondered what he had been doing all the time she had been away. Probably found a nice girl, married her and settled down to farming, she thought. Something deep inside of her hurt at the thought. She would rather imagine that Helmut would be with Tina and Papa in Texas, waiting for her.

The trouble with me, Louisa thought, dismayed at facing the truth about herself, is that I want everything! I want adventure and a carefree life, but I also want love and someone to love me . . . and, yes, a family to take care of and watch grow. I doubt if any man would have me, after the way I've been living these past months. I can imagine what the women in Fredericksburg will say when they learn I've been in the army, a male orderly at that!

Louisa shrugged her shoulders. Let whatever happens be, she thought. I would not trade these past months for anything . . . even with the lice and tics and filth and bad food and, yes, typhoid! When I cared for those sick soldiers, I felt as though I was really doing something worthwhile and important. How can I ever match that feeling by being a housewife and tending babies?

As the days passed, Will regained his strength little by little. His spirits seemed to be healing, too. Louisa felt sure that when they reached Jefferson and he saw Tina and Papa, he would become the old Will she had always loved.

He said very little about the battles he had seen or about the war. He said nothing about Melissa. Instead he spent his time remembering the old days and the good times the family had known. He was able to talk about Fred now, and that was good, Louisa thought. Yes, Will would be all right. She wished she were as sure of her own future.

Then, they were there: Jefferson, Texas. They had crossed Arkansas by back roads, the long, slow but safe way. And it had worked. Louisa's heart beat faster as Will guided the horses toward the hotel. What if they weren't there? What if Fritz what's-his-name didn't give them her message? What if . . . ?

Will pulled the wagon up in front of the hotel and jumped down, his hand reaching for Louisa's. She joined him, glad to feel Texas earth beneath her feet again.

"Do you think they'll be here, Will?" she asked, so nervous her teeth chattered.

"Well, little sister, let's go find out," Will said, with some of his old charm returned.

She followed Will into the hotel, adjusting her bonnet and smoothing out the wrinkles in the dull, brown dress. She must look a sight.

At the registration desk Will spoke to the clerk. "Do you have a Herr von Scholl registered here? Max von Scholl?"

The clerk checked his big, black leather book. Under his eyeshade his face shown green.

"No, sir, I don't have anyone by that name here. Do you wish to register?" He turned the book towards Will and handed him a pen. Will glanced at Louisa, a question in his eyes.

"Is there another hotel in town?" she asked the clerk. "We really need to find Herr von Scholl." Her spirits sank as she talked. What if they weren't here? What if something had happened to them?

"Yes, there are four," the clerk said, a disapproving frown replacing his previous thin smile. "This is by far the best of the lot, however, ma'am."

"Thank you. We may be back." Louisa grabbed Will's arm, and they rushed out to the wagon. "It's getting late, and I'm so tired. Let's hurry and find them, so we can settle in." She didn't mention her fears to Will.

All three remaining hotel clerks, differing only in size and shape but not in attitude, said no, there was no Max von Scholl at their hotels.

Dejected, her disappointment almost a physical pain, Louisa sat in the wagon, wondering what to do next. Will had become very quiet, as though waiting for Louisa to decide.

Louisa sat bolt upright, her face alight. "Will, let's start all over at the first hotel. They probably were afraid to use Papa's German name and registered under Robinson. Hurry, I know they'll be there!"

And they were. The clerk immediately recognized the name Mrs. Jeffrey Robinson. She and her papa, very nice people, had been here for a week, he said, waiting for someone. Room 212. . . . Louisa didn't wait to hear more. She lifted up her skirts and flew up the stairs and down the hall . . . Room 212!

She knocked, twice, then again. "Just a minute, please," came from within . . . Tina's voice! Her sister! Hurry up, Tina, open the door!

The door opened a few inches, then was flung wide.

"Louisa! Papa, come see, it's Louisa, back safe and sound." She pulled Louisa into the room, and they fell into each others arms, laughing and crying.

"Ah, Louisa," said Papa as he joined them, leaning heavily on a cane, "how good it is to see you at last. We have worried so about you!"

"Papa!" Louisa kissed her father's cheek and took his hands in hers. "Come, see the surprise I have for you."

"Louisa . . . is it . . . I mean . . . did you . . . ?" Papa stammered. I have never heard him like this, Louisa thought. He's so afraid to hope that Will is here.

159

Then Will walked into the room. Both Papa and Tina stood, unable to move, staring at the son and brother they had thought never to see again.

Tears and laughter. How close they are to one another, Louisa thought later, after all the greetings had been said, the tears shed and the laughter rung out like music in the little room. For a few moments there was nothing in that room but pure joy!

Louisa felt a pang of disappointment. Helmut. He hadn't come with the others to meet her. He'd probably forgotten all about her by now. She wanted to cry . . . or to run away.

"Tina," she said, needing to know, "how is Helmut these days? Is he married? I hope he is well." She tried, not quite succeeding, to sound casual.

"Ach, Louisa," Tina exclaimed, "I did forget! I have a letter for you from Helmut. He wrote it several months ago, before he went away."

Louisa turned away so that Tina couldn't see the tears that welled up in her eyes. So he hadn't waited to see if she would come home. He had left . . . several months ago! Well, at least now she knew.

"Louisa? Don't you want to read Helmut's letter?" Tina asked, holding the envelope out to Louisa.

"Yes, I'll read it," Louisa said, her heart aching as she tore open the envelope and read aloud.

"*Dearest Louisa, You must pardon the riting and mostly the speling. i don't rite english so good,*" Louisa read aloud. She looked up at Papa and Tina who were watching her closely. Her eyes dropped back to the letter.

"*i don't know when you will reseave this letter. i am riting it the night before i leave for New Orleans. You have been gon for one week alredy . . .* " One week? He only waited one week before he left? Oooh! . . ."*and i miss you vary mush . . .* " But not enough to wait? Oh, Helmut! "*enyway, i could not stay here and no that you are in so mush danger. It would*

160

rite. so i leave to join the Yankee Army . . ." The army? Gentle
Helmut in the army? Louisa couldn't imagine such a thing.
*"and i don't no when i retern, or if i retern. So i must put in
my por riting how i feel so you will no.*

*"i want you should be my wife, Louisa, if i come back from
the war. . . ."* Louisa gulped and felt her face turning fiery
red. Without glancing at her eager audience, she turned
her back and continued reading to herself.

*"i have luved you sinse i first saw you, standing over me
in the wuds. Surely you no this, i am not gud at hiding my
felings.*

*"You do not have to anser this leter, becuase i do not no
where i will be by the time you get it. Just remember, i luv you.
plese wate for me. Sined, your servent, Helmut."*

Louisa sat down on the nearest chair with a thud. She
couldn't believe her eyes. Never in the world did she expect
such feelings from Helmut. They were such good friends.
And yet? Hadn't she felt deserted and heartsick when she
thought he had gone from her? Was that just for a lost
friend? She would have no sleep this night, thinking of
Helmut and his letter and wondering about her own feelings.

"Well, Louisa, you surely shut us out in a hurry!"
Tina said, laughing at Tina's blush. "What else did he say?
Don't leave us like this!"

"You heard," Louisa said, blushing. "He wants me to
marry him when he returns from the war."

"Well? Well?" Tina's voice insisted. "What do you think?
How do you feel? Will you marry him?"

"Oh, Tina, I don't know. This is all too much. Coming
home and being a girl . . . a woman . . . again after so long
at play-acting. I'm so confused. I'll just have to do a lot of
thinking!"

"That is *gut*, Louisa," Papa said from his chair, "I
think you should think long and hard before making such

an important decision. You have grown into a fine young woman and my dearest wish is for your life-long happiness. Ja."

Papa nodded his head and retreated into his chair. The effort it took to make his little speech seemed to have tired him. Louisa covered his legs with a small blanket and kissed his forehead.

"I love you, Papa," she said. "And now I intend to take a bath in that wonderful copper tub in the bathroom!"

They decided to remain in Jefferson for a day or two to give Will and Louisa a rest from their long trip before starting out for Fredericksburg. Louisa luxuriated in the hotel's hot bath and a real bed! But every waking moment she spent pondering her life and what she should do with it. Being grown up had turned out to be a very difficult thing!

The seed of the idea grew slowly. She knew it was there, but she left it alone, to come out only when it was ready. Like an egg hatching, she thought, or a baby being born.

One morning she woke up with a big smile on her face. At first she thought she must have had a particularly happy dream. Then she remembered. In the middle of the night it had come to her. She knew what she wanted to do!

After breakfasting in the hotel dining room — their gold coins were almost gone — the family went back to Room 212 to pack; it was time to go home.

Tina pulled a small fabric case out from under the bed. "Here, Louisa, I brought some of your clothes along. I didn't know you'd be clever enough to get some yourself."

"Oh, Tina, how wonderful! I do need them. Everyone listen. This is what Louisa Emily von Scholl, the former Louis Emil Robinson, is going to do.

"When you leave for Fredericksburg today, I will not be going with you." Tina, Will and Papa gasped, as though they were one person.

"What do you mean, Louisa? Of course you're going home with us!" Tina said, a hurt tone in her voice, as if to say, "How could you possibly consider anything else?"

"No, I mean it, Tina," Louisa said. "I have been thinking about my life and what I want most to do. And I am going to offer my services as a nurse, wherever anyone needs me."

"A nurse?" Will spoke up. "But, Louisa, you have given so much to the war already. All those hard months of saving soldiers' lives. Isn't that enough? Wouldn't you like to settle down, at home, where it's safe now?"

"Yes, Will, I would love to feel safe again. But I don't expect to until this war is over, one way or the other. And I won't feel comfortable if I'm not doing what I can to help the wounded and sick boys who are fighting for us . . . on either side.

"I reckon I'll volunteer at a Confederate hospital, since Miss Dorothea Dix won't let a nurse under thirty years of age near her Yankee boys. I'm sure the Confederates won't hold it against me that I'm only sixteen!

"After all, Will was a rebel and my dear friend, George, a dyed-in-the-wool Yankee. Fred was against the war altogether, and died for his beliefs as surely as any soldier.

"Papa," Louisa said, tears in her voice, "is it not so, that all sides in war believe they are right — and all sides, in the end, are wrong? It really doesn't matter, does it, Papa? The Yankee soldiers I nursed were as bloody and as dead as Will's Confederate friends. As dead as our dear Fred. Nothing changes that, does it, Papa?"

"Nein, my dear daughter, nothing changes that."

Afterword

When one thinks of a historical novel, two things come to mind. First, "novel" conjures images of fictional people, places and things. But, "historical" says to the reader: facts, dates, real places. How can one book do both?

That very problem makes writing historical novels rewarding to the author and, hopefully, fascinating to the reader.

I would like to point out a few places where I used factual material to make my fiction come alive:

Fredericksberg, Texas, and all the other locations in the book are real places. Some of the action in those places was based on history, some is pure fiction.

Most of the German people in Gillespie County and neighboring Hill Country counties were against slavery, and ninety-six percent voted against seceding from the Union. As a result, they were subject to many hardships, including the Nueces Massacre which really happened on August 9, 1862. Years later a monument to the men who died there was erected in Comfort, Texas. It reads *Treu der Union* (True to the Union).

Both battles of Corinth and the siege of Vicksburg are documented, as were the activities of the Second Texas Infantry.

When Louisa donned a soldier's uniform and went off to war, she was only one of over 800 women, on both sides, who actually did the same. Some were never found out, others sent home. A few even won medals, and one was awarded a federal veteran's pension after the war.

Bibliography

Biesele, Rudolph Leopold. *The History of the German Settlements in Texas: 1831-1861.* (Austin, Texas: Press of Von Boeckmann-Jones Co., n.d.)

Biggers, Don H. ed. *German Pioneers in Texas.* (Fredericksburg, Texas: Fredericksburg Publishing Co., 1925)

Catton, Bruce. *Grant Moves South.* (Boston: Little, Brown and Co., 1960)

Chance, Joseph E. *The Second Texas Infantry.* (Austin, Texas: Eakin Press, 1984)

Commager, Henry Steele, ed. *The Blue and the Gray,* Vol. II. (Indianapolis: Bobbs-Merrill Co., Inc., 1950)

Dannett, Sylvia G. L. *Noble Women of the North.* (New York: Thomas Yoseloff, 1959)

Diamond Jubilee Souvenir Book of Comfort, Texas. (San Antonio: Standard Printing, 1929)

Edmonds, S. Emma E. *Nurse and Spy in the Union Army.* (Hartford, Conn.: W. S. Williams & Co., 1865)

Federal Writers' Project of the Works Progress Administration. *Mississippi: A Guide to the Magnolia State.* (New York: Hastings House, 1928)

Fishbein's Illustrated Medical and Health Encyclopedia, v. 21. (Westport, Conn: H.S.Stuttman Inc., 1981)

Gordon, Alice, et al. *Smithsonian Guide to Historic America.* (New York: Stewart, Tabori and Chang, 1990)

Goyne, Minetta Altgelt. *Lone Star and Double Eagle, Civil War Letters of a German-Texas Family.* (Fort Worth, Texas: Texas Christian University Press, 1982)

Greene, Francis Vinton. *The Mississippi.* (New York: Jack Brussel, n.d.)

Jandad, Ulrich. *The New Goat Handbook.* (New York: Barron's, 1987)

Korn, Jerry. *War on the Mississippi.* (Alexandria, Va.: Time-Life Books Inc., 1985)

Marten, James. *Texas Divided: Loyalty and Dissent in the Lone Star State, 1856-1874.* (Lexington: University Press of Kentucky)

Massey, Mary Elizabeth. *Ersatz in the Confederacy.* (Columbia: University of South Carolina Press, 1952)

Milhollen, Hirst Dillon and James Ralph Johnson. *Best Photos of the Civil War.* (New York: ARCO, 1981)

Miller, Ray. *Eyes of Texas Travel Guide.* (Houston, Texas: Cordovan Corp., 1980)

Robinson, Victor. *White Caps: The Story of Nursing.* (Philadelphia: J. B. Lippincott Co., 1946)

Staubing, Harold Elk. *Civil War Eyewitness Reports.* (Connecticut: Archon Books, 1985)

Stern, Philip Van Doren. *Soldier Life in the Union and Confederate Armies.* (Bloomington: Indiana University Press, 1961)

Sutherland, Daniel E. *The Expansion of Everyday Life, 1860-1876.* (New York: Harper & Row, 1989)

Wiggins, William H. Jr. *O Freedom!* (Tennessee: University of Tennessee, 1987)

Wiley, Bell Irvin. *The Life of Johnny Reb, The Common Soldier of the Confederacy.* (New York: The Bobbs-Merrill Company, 1943)

_____. *The Life of Billy Yank, the Common Soldier of the Union.* (New York: The Bobbs-Merrill Company, 1951)

Williams, R. H. *With the Border Ruffians: Memories of the Far West, 1852-1868.* (Toronto: The Musson Book Co., Ltd., 1919)

Wortham, Louis J. *A History of Texas: From Wilderness to Commonwealth.* (Fort Worth, Texas: Wortham-Molyneaux Company, 1924)

Young, Agatha. *The Women and the Crisis.* (New York: McDowell, Obolensky, 1959)

Zelade, Richard. *Hill Country: Discovering the Secrets of the Texas Hill Country.* (Austin: Texas Monthly Press, 1987)

The Author

Raised in Idaho and Indiana, Marj Gurasich has been a resident of the Houston area for over thirty years. Her other novels include *Red Wagons and White, Benito and the White Dove,* and *Letters to Oma.* She is also the author of the nonfiction book, *Did You Ever Meet a Texas Hero?*

Of German descent herself, Ms. Gurasich visited the Texas Hill Country several times researching the background for *A House Divided.*